True Love

Amber got in line at the pencil sharpener. David Jackson saw her and left his seat to stand in line behind her.

Amber's heart pounded. She knew David didn't need to sharpen his pencil. He just wanted to stand next to her.

"Amber, I have to tell you something," he whispered.

"What?" she whispered back. It was her turn at the pencil sharpener. She stuck her pencil in the hole and turned the crank very slowly.

"I . . . uh . . . you know I like you, Amber," he stammered. "A lot. And I think you like me, too. Right?"

"Yes, I like you." Actually, the warm-vegetable-soup feeling she had for David was stronger than like. But she didn't want to tell David she loved him until he said it first.

"Well . . . uh . . . I think . . . we ought to . . . will you marry me?"

Tales From Third Grade

Why Are Boys So Weird?

Candice F. Ransom

Troll Associates

Why Are Boys So Weird?

ONE

While her teacher was reading a story about Paul Bunyan to her third grade class, Amber Cantrell was making envelopes for her Valentine party invitations.

She was supposed to be paying attention, not making envelopes. But it was not unusual for Amber to be doing something else while she was supposed to be listening. Her older brother, Justin, didn't call her Ants-in-the-Pants Amber for nothing.

The story Mrs. Sharp was reading was very exciting. Paul Bunyan was a huge lumberjack who had a giant blue ox named Babe. The class laughed loudly at the part about Paul Bunyan's giant flapjack griddle.

Amber used that laughter to cover the sound of her ripping a second piece of construction paper along the edge of her desk. It would have been easier to use scissors, but Mrs. Sharp would have seen the silver metal flashing.

She began folding the sheets into envelopes. Her invitations were really cute, she thought, tucking one into the first completed envelope.

In the center of a red paper heart, she had pasted a white arrow. On the arrow was written, *"My heart will be broken if you don't come to my Valentine's Day tea party. Bring your best stuffed animal."* Around the rim of the heart, she had printed the date and time of the party. She was having her party on Sunday, the day before Valentine's Day.

She didn't have to put her name and address on the invitations. Only two people were being invited and they knew about the party already. Amber liked to do things right, so she insisted on making invitations.

Now Mrs. Sharp was telling about the Blue Snowstorm, during which all the snow that fell was bright blue. Amber thought blue snow sounded very pretty.

Delight Wakefield raised her hand. "How could Paul find his blue ox in a blue snowstorm?"

"Good question, Delight," Mrs. Sharp said. "Class, can you think of any other problems one might have with blue snow?"

Mindy Alexander, Amber's best friend, said, "You wouldn't be able to tell the sky from the ground if everything was blue."

"Yeah!" agreed David Jackson. "You'd get dizzy!"

Amber looked over at David. He was wearing a red sweater and his cheeks were still red from playing outside. His hair stood up in a cowlick. David was Amber's on-again, off-again boyfriend. Sometimes she liked him. Sometimes she wished he was on another planet.

But not today. Today she thought he looked really cute, with his cowlick and red sweater. She almost wished she had invited him to her party.

The class began chattering about what it would be like to have blue snow.

"My dad says it's supposed to snow this weekend," said Carly. "Wouldn't it be funny if it snowed *blue*?"

"You could have blue snow slushies whenever you wanted," exclaimed Henry Hoffstedder. "Throw blue snowballs at stupid girls like Amber Cantrell!"

Amber frowned. Even though Henry sat on the other side of the room, she heard his remark. Henry was the reason she couldn't invite David to her party. David would probably want to bring that awful Henry Hoffstedder. Amber didn't want her party wrecked.

Anyway, her party wasn't the kind you could invite boys to. It was a tea party. She was inviting her best-best friend, Mindy Alexander, and her second-best friend, Delight Wakefield. And their stuffed animals.

Amber still played with her stuffed raccoon, R.C.

Her father had given her the raccoon for her sixth birthday, right before he moved out. R.C. was her most prized possession in the world.

"I'd make a blue snowman," said Delight. "The biggest snowman ever!"

"You couldn't make a snowman that big," said David, who sat right behind her.

"Could, too!" Delight stuck her tongue out at him.

David laughed.

Watching them, Amber frowned again. Although she liked Delight, she didn't like David Jackson paying attention to her. He was *her* on-again, off-again boyfriend, not Delight's.

"All right, class, simmer down," Mrs. Sharp said, going to the light switch to flick it on and off. That was the signal to be quiet. She continued with the story of Paul Bunyan.

"According to the legend, the Blue Snowstorm occurred during the Year of Two Winters. That year it was so cold, they had winter all summer. Paul put the coffeepot outside to cool and the coffee froze so fast, the ice was *hot*."

Amber whispered across the aisle to Mindy, "Wouldn't it be neat to have two winters, with tons of snow and lots of days off from school?"

Mindy nodded. "Even *one* winter would be nice."

So far this winter, it had only snowed once—a

skimpy snow that had barely covered the ground. True, they had had no school that day, but it wasn't much fun. There wasn't enough snow to go sledding or to build a decent snowman. Amber had spent the entire afternoon scraping snow and rolling it into fist-sized balls for a small snowman. Justin had laughed at the sight of Amber's stunted snowman.

A snowy Valentine's Day would be great, she thought now. She pictured big, lazy flakes falling among the trees. She liked the idea of everything white and lacy, like an old-fashioned Valentine.

Mrs. Sharp began another Paul Bunyan tale. This one was about a giant cornstalk he grew. Amber only half-listened. Mrs. Sharp had been reading aloud stories about folk heroes the last few days.

Yesterday they'd heard the legend of Pecos Bill. He was a super-cowboy with a horse named Widow Maker. The day before that, they'd heard about Mike Fink. Both of these characters performed fantastic deeds.

Amber wasn't much interested in how Paul Bunyan logged the whole state of North Dakota. She put her head down on her desk, stretching her arms beneath. Her forearm brushed something scratchy. She reached around and pulled it free.

It was a purple plastic strip, the kind that people used to label suitcases and radios with their names. The raised letters spelled out "FWR '79." Amber studied the inscription, wondering what it meant. She didn't know why the strip was on the underside of her desk, but she put it back, pressing the plastic firmly until it stuck fast again.

"Pssst." Amber tried to get Mindy's attention to show her friend her discovery.

But Mindy was listening to the story.

Amber went back to her envelopes. She wrote Mindy's name on one and Delight's name on the other. Her invitations were finished.

She should wait until library period to hand the invitations to Mindy and Delight. But she didn't want to wait.

Passing notes in Room Six was strictly forbidden. But she wasn't as worried about breaking the rules as she'd been at the beginning of the year. As the year had gone on, Amber had grown more daring.

She would be careful. Mrs. Sharp wouldn't see her pass the envelopes. Like Paul Bunyan or Pecos Bill, Amber Gillian Cantrell could do the impossible.

Mindy's desk was right next to Amber's. Amber waited until Mrs. Sharp was turning a page, then quickly plopped the envelope on Mindy's desk.

Mindy smoothly palmed the envelope off her desk and into her lap. She opened it quietly and eased out the red heart. She smiled and nodded at Amber to let her know she would be at Amber's party.

Mindy Alexander had moved into the house across

from Amber's the day Amber's father had moved out of the Cantrell house. While her parents were getting divorced, Amber had needed a friend.

She and Mindy had started school together at Virginia Run Elementary. They had been in the same class since first grade. Amber and Mindy did everything together. Mindy was always invited to Amber's parties.

One envelope down, one to go.

Delivering Delight's invitation was trickier. Delight sat on the far side of the classroom. Her invitation would have farther to travel.

Amber dropped the envelope on Carly's desk, signaling Carly to pass it on.

Carly slid the envelope onto Lisa's desk. So far, so good.

Delight was looking at Amber, waiting for the envelope to land on her desk. Amber gave her a thumb's-up salute.

Delight Wakefield had moved to the neighborhood last summer. She was the new girl in Mrs. Sharp's class. At first Amber didn't like Delight. Before Delight came, Amber was the most popular girl in her class. She had a pretty name and long hair she could almost sit on.

But then Delight had shown up. Her name was prettier than Amber's and she *could* sit on her hair. Delight had also lived in Paris, France.

The other kids liked Delight better than they liked Amber. David Jackson teased Delight more than he teased Amber. Even Mindy was fascinated by Delight. Amber was jealous of the new girl.

One day a few months ago, Amber had grabbed a pair of scissors and cut a piece of Delight's beautiful waist-length hair. Delight's hair was ruined. She had to have it cut short.

Amber had felt so bad, she gave Delight her most prized possession, her stuffed raccoon. But Delight would not take R.C. Eventually the girls patched up their differences and became friends.

Amber checked the progress of Delight's invitation. Mrs. Sharp was still reading.

Henry Hoffstedder turned around. He saw the invitation land on the desk behind his.

"Hey, Mrs. Sharp!" Henry blurted.

Mrs. Sharp looked at him. "What is it, Henry?" Her tone implied his reason for the interruption had better be good.

Amber froze. Henry was going to tell her about the invitation!

"Something bit me," he said, to Amber's relief. "My arm itches. Can I go to the nurse's office?"

Mrs. Sharp walked down the aisle to inspect Henry's arm. Amber's heart bumped. The invitation was in plain sight, right behind Henry.

"This is a very tiny mark, Henry," the teacher

said. "I think you'll live until the last bell." She went back to the front to resume reading.

Now the invitation was making its perilous way onto David Jackson's desk. One more desk to go before it reached Delight. Amber crossed her fingers.

David held the invitation up close to his nose, as if he had trouble reading the name printed on the envelope. Then he held it far away, wrinkling his nose, as if it smelled.

Just give the envelope to Delight! Amber thought desperately.

Then David passed the envelope under the seat of Delight's desk, to avoid being seen. A second later, Mrs. Sharp swooped down and took the envelope.

"I'll have that, please," she said to David.

Amber slumped in her seat. She knew what would happen next.

TWO

Putting her book down once more, Mrs. Sharp opened Delight's invitation.

"You know the rules," she said sternly. "Any notes retrieved by me will be read aloud in class. I hope for your sake, David, that this isn't a mushy love letter."

The class laughed. Henry Hoffstedder laughed louder than anyone.

"I didn't send it!" David protested. "I was just passing it!"

Mrs. Sharp took out the red heart and read, " 'My heart will be broken if you don't come to my Valentine's Day tea party. Bring your best stuffed animal.' " She turned the heart over. "No name. I guess the party-giver wants to remain anonymous."

"Awww!" Henry jeered. "I didn't know you were

having a tea party, David. How come you didn't invite me?"

"It's Amber's party!" David cried. "I heard her and Mindy talking about it. She's only inviting Mindy and Delight. And their goofy stuffed animals."

Amber's face went as red as her heart-shaped invitation. Now everyone knew that she was having a tea party for stuffed animals. And that she was only inviting two kids out of her class.

Carly turned to Amber. "Why didn't you invite me?" she said accusingly.

"Or me?" asked Lisa.

Carly and Lisa sat at Amber's table during lunch. Amber liked them as school friends, but not as *best* friends. Only best friends were being invited to her party. But she still didn't want to hurt anyone's feelings.

"I want to come, too!" Henry demanded.

"Me, too!" David chimed in. "I'll bring my snake, Titus. He's not stuffed, but he doesn't eat much."

The boys cracked up.

Mrs. Sharp flicked the lights on and off angrily. "You can certainly tell it's Friday in here. Your bonus library period is about to go out the window. I suggest you settle down."

If they behaved during the week, the third-graders earned an extra library period on Fridays. Now that they were this close to gaining the privilege, they didn't want to lose it. The class became quiet.

Mrs. Sharp went to the board and began writing.

"Your assignment over the next several weeks is to write your own legend," she said. "I want you to create your own folk hero, like Paul Bunyan or Pecos Bill."

Mindy made a face at Amber. "That sounds hard," she whispered.

Amber knew Mindy didn't like creative assignments. Mindy was good at practical things, like math and sports. Amber liked to make things, like tiny magazines for R.C. But making up stories was another matter. She wished she had paid more attention when the teacher had read about Paul Bunyan and Pecos Bill.

"The librarian will show you more books about folk heroes. I'll answer questions when we come back," Mrs. Sharp said. "Let's line up and walk to the library in an orderly manner, please."

As they filed down the hall, Amber poked David Jackson in the back. She didn't think he looked so cute in his red sweater now.

"Thanks for getting me in trouble," she said.

"You're welcome," he said grandly. He and Henry Hoffstedder laughed until Mrs. Sharp shot them a dark look.

Delight was in line behind Amber. "Thanks for the invitation. It's Sunday, right? I'll be there." She pointed to David and Henry. "Aren't boys the weirdest things on earth?"

"You said it," Amber agreed. "I'm glad I'm not a boy."

In the library, Amber led her friends to a table by the window. The librarian began talking to the class.

"Your teacher tells me you will all be writing your own legends," said Miss Maddox. "Does anyone know what a legend is?"

Carly raised her hand. "It's a story about a famous person. Sometimes he's really big, like Paul Bunyan. Sometimes he's regular size, like Pecos Bill."

"Is this famous person real?" asked Miss Maddox.

"No," answered David Jackson.

"Yes," said Amber at the same time.

"David says the folk hero is not real. Amber says he is," Miss Maddox said. "Class, who do you think is right?"

Immediately the girls sided with Amber.

"Amber is right!" Delight cried.

The boys booed the girls.

"Do you think Paul Bunyan was *real*?" Henry scoffed. "He was a giant! Amber believes in giants!" The other boys hooted with laughter.

"Pecos Bill could have been a real person!" Amber insisted. "He wasn't a giant!"

"He lassoed a cyclone!" Henry said. "Nobody could do that!"

Amber blushed. This was not her day. First David had gotten her in trouble. Now Henry was making her look like an idiot.

Miss Maddox spoke up. "Let me ask you boys something. Do any of you read super-hero comics? Or watch movies about super heroes?"

"You bet," replied Henry.

"Do you believe that those super-hero characters exist?" the librarian asked. "Are they real?"

"Yeah," David answered. Then he added quickly, "No. I don't know. Maybe."

Henry said, "It isn't the same thing! Paul Bunyan and those guys were back in the olden days. They weren't real."

"And your super heroes are?" Miss Maddox smiled. "Did you know that the first Superman comic came out in the 1930s? I'm sure to you guys, the thirties are the olden days."

No one commented on this. Amber used the small silence to stick out her tongue at Henry Hoffstedder. Boys didn't know everything!

"A folk hero," Miss Maddox explained, "is someone who is larger than life. He does things a normal person couldn't possibly do. He doesn't have to be a giant like Paul Bunyan. He can seem like a normal person, like Clark Kent before he turns into Superman. He can be a cowboy or a turtle with special powers."

Amber raised her hand. "Do folk heroes always have to be boys?"

"Absolutely not. Remember Paul Bunyan's wife?" The librarian opened a book. "It took thirteen Hudson's Bay blankets to make Mrs. Bunyan's skirt. And an extra-big moose hide for each of her shoes. She could toss rocks and logs to dam up a river and split more rails than any three men."

She told them more about legends and folk heroes. Then the class was allowed to look for books.

Amber found a book that seemed interesting. As she reached for the shelf, a hand shot out and snatched the very book Amber wanted.

It was David.

"I saw that book first!" Amber cried. "Give it back!"

"I was faster," David said, holding the book up high.

"I'll tell Miss Maddox."

He grinned. "So tell her. But I got there first." He left to check out the book.

David had been hanging around Henry Hoffstedder too much, Amber thought, fuming. He was just as awful as Henry.

She saw David accidentally bump into Delight, then heard him tell Delight he was sorry.

Amber crossed her arms angrily. David apologized for bumping into Delight, but he had treated Amber rudely. If he didn't watch it, she was going to find herself another boy to like!

Suddenly Amber remembered the mysterious plastic strip under her desk. She walked over to the librarian to ask her about it.

"Yes, Amber?" Miss Maddox said.

"I found something under my desk," Amber said. She described the purple plastic strip with its strange letters and numbers. "Do you know what it means?"

" 'FWR' are initials," Miss Maddox explained. "And ' '79' stands for the year 1979. A student with the initials FWR probably sat in your desk in 1979. I would guess FWR put the strip under the desk on purpose."

"But why?"

"So he or she would be remembered. To let the world know he or she was there, back in 1979. Someday, somebody would find the strip and wonder about that person, just as you did."

"Do you know who FWR was?" Amber asked.

The librarian shook her head. "I wasn't working in this school in 1979. But I have met a lot of memorable students!"

Amber went back to her table. She considered telling Mindy and Delight about her discovery. Then she decided to keep the purple plastic strip a secret.

Some boy or girl stuck the plastic strip under her desk, just to be remembered. That person must have known that one day, years later, some other third-grader would find the strip.

Amber thought about her third grade year so far. She was one of the most popular kids in her class. Everyone knew who she was. But she would only be in Mrs. Sharp's room another couple of months.

Then summer vacation would come. Next fall, Amber would be in fourth grade, in another class. Suppose everyone forgot who she was?

How could she be remembered?

Library period was nearly over. Miss Maddox had them line up at the door to go back to Room Six. "Walk quietly down the hall. Other classes are in session. You don't want to disturb them."

"Yes, we do," someone blurted at the end of the line.

Amber recognized Henry Hoffstedder's voice.

So did the librarian.

"Henry," she warned. "Do you want me to send a note to your teacher?"

"Yeah! Tell her how smart I am!" But he didn't say it very loud.

As they left the library, Amber heard Miss Maddox mutter to her aide, "That Henry! His mouth is legendary!"

Henry's mouth was a legend! This was news to Amber. She had no idea ordinary kids could be legends.

Henry's mouth could be a folk hero, she thought, smothering a giggle. She pictured Henry's lips doing impossible folk-hero tasks, like splitting rails and lassoing a cyclone. Her giggles burst out.

"What's so funny?" Mindy said, turning around.

"Tell you later," Amber whispered.

She wondered if she should tell Henry he wouldn't have to make up a folk hero for his legend assignment. He could write about his mouth! Henry was probably one of those memorable kids Miss Maddox was talking about.

Amber longed to be a memorable student, a third-grader people would talk about for years to come.

Then she had an idea. Since ordinary people could be a legend, why couldn't *she* be one, too? Why not write about herself?

She would be Amber Gillian Cantrell, Third Grade Legend.

Chapter

THREE

The morning of her party, Amber woke up and listened. It was strangely silent outside. Not just the usual Sunday morning quiet, but a different stillness. . . .

She sat up and looked out her window.

It was snowing!

Huge, fluffy flakes drifted past the window. The tops of the cars and shrubs were already coated white.

"It's snowing!" Amber yelled, bounding out of bed.

Her older brother, Justin, poked his head out of his own doorway.

"Of course it's snowing," he said in that superior tone that drove Amber crazy. "It's been snowing for *hours*. Everybody knows that but you. If you'd get up earlier—"

"Oh, who cares?" Amber hurriedly pulled on pants and a sweater. She was too excited to let her brother aggravate her.

She ran into the kitchen. Breakfast was on the table.

Mrs. Cantrell was looking through a carton of old quilts she had bought at an estate sale the day before. She owned a shop where she sold old and new handmade quilts. The store was called A Stitch in Time.

"Mom!" Amber cried. "It's snowing! Isn't it neat for Valentine's Day? Everything looks all white and pretty, like a Valentine!"

Her mother poured Amber a glass of juice. "Why, Amber, you're a romantic. I never realized that before."

Amber helped herself to a cinnamon bun. "What's a romantic?" she asked, her mouth full.

"It means you like romance. You like things that are pretty and old-fashioned and traditional."

"Isn't romance about love?" Amber wondered.

"Yes, it is." Her mother smiled. "You might say a romantic is someone who loves love."

Justin came in, dressed for sledding. "Don't put ideas into her head, Mom. Amber's mushy enough as it is."

Justin grabbed the last cinnamon roll in his gloved hand and went outdoors before she could think of a really good remark to fire back.

"He makes me so mad," Amber told her mother.

"Don't tell Justin I said this," Mrs. Cantrell said, "but he's a romantic, too."

"*Justin* loves love?" Amber couldn't believe it. Not her thirteen-year-old brother! He only seemed to like rock music and lifting weights in the basement.

"He wouldn't admit it in a million years, but, yes, your brother gets mushy over sunsets and snowfalls. The other day I saw him in the drugstore, picking out a fancy Valentine card. And it wasn't for me."

"Then who was it for?"

"Obviously a girl he likes," her mother replied.

This was news to Amber. "Justin has a *girlfriend*?"

"Well, he is almost fourteen." Her mother went back to sorting quilts. "Look at this one. It's called a charm quilt."

Amber touched the soft, worn fabric sewn into dozens of tiny squares. She handled the quilt gently, knowing it was very old and probably worth a lot of money.

"It's nice," she said, "but what's so special about it?"

Her mother held up the quilt. "Look at the squares. The material is all different. No two patches were cut from the same piece of cloth."

Amber studied the quilt and could not find two pieces of the same fabric.

"There are 999 blocks in a charm quilt," her mother said. "In the old days, a girl made a charm quilt to find her true love."

"How?" asked Amber. Sewing a quilt didn't seem like a very good way to find a boyfriend.

"Well, when she finished sewing the last block, number 999, her true love was supposed to come along. The fabric of his coat would make the thousandth patch."

"Really?" Amber looked respectfully at the quilt. "Is that true?"

"It's folklore, an old tale," her mother said. "But those old tales started somewhere, back in a time when people believed in such things. Who knows? It might be true."

This was a different kind of story than the tall tales Amber had heard in school. Her head whirled with images of Paul Bunyan and blue snow and a quilt that could find a person's true love.

Preparations for Amber's party began right after lunch.

"I'm out of here," Justin said, when Mrs. Cantrell asked him to help frost the cookies. He jammed his stocking hat on his head and went back outside to work on his snow fort.

"We don't need boys around anyway," Amber said, spreading pink icing on a heart-shaped cookie. "This is for girls only."

"Yes," her mother agreed. "I guess a tea party is too frilly for boys."

There was a knock at the back door. Mrs. Wakefield came in, stomping snow from her boots. Her arms were filled with bags.

Mrs. Wakefield was Delight's mother. She was also Mrs. Cantrell's business partner. Together, the two women worked in the quilt shop. Mrs. Wakefield had come over to help decorate for the party.

"Hello, Amber. Hello, Louise," she said to Mrs. Cantrell. "Let's get this party rolling!"

Out of the mysterious bags came wonderful things—gold-rimmed china cups and saucers, silver candlesticks, a teapot shaped like a cottage. There were old-fashioned Valentine cards constructed of lacy layers. Amber pulled out one to reveal a scene of a boat on a lake. Another showed a girl in a swing.

"Where did all this stuff come from?" Mrs. Cantrell asked.

Delight's mother laughed. "I've been collecting junk since I was Amber's age. I went to a garage sale when I was eight and bought a china cat. Then I had to have *another* china cat."

Amber picked up a shiny silver spoon. She wouldn't call the things Mrs. Wakefield collected junk. Maybe she would start going to garage sales herself, to see what interesting things she could find.

Her mother and Mrs. Wakefield went into the dining room.

"Don't peek," Mrs. Cantrell warned her.

Amber went into her room to change. Her mother had laid out her white party dress and white tights. Amber was slipping into her shiny white shoes when her mother came in to fix her hair.

"Don't you want to cut this mop?" Mrs. Cantrell teased, tying a white satin ribbon in Amber's ponytail. Amber's stuffed raccoon, R.C., wore a red satin ribbon around his neck.

"Never!" Amber said, tossing her head. Her hair was almost long enough to sit on. "I want my hair to grow down to the floor!"

"Won't that be a nuisance?" her mother said. "Stepping on your own hair all the time?"

"Oh, Mom!"

The doorbell rang. Amber's party guests had arrived.

Amber grabbed R.C. off the bed and ran to answer the door.

Mindy and Delight came in, making a little snowfall on the rug as they took off their coats. They carried their stuffed animals in plastic bags.

Mindy wore a pink ruffled dress and ruffly pink socks to match. She held Pearl, her stuffed penguin.

"I love your dress," Amber said to her.

"I like yours, too," Mindy said.

Delight took her stuffed dog, Row-bear, from the

bag. Row-bear came all the way from Paris, France. Delight had on a red velvet dress and tiny earrings with real red stones.

"They were my grandmother's," she said. "They're rubies."

"Wow!" Amber exclaimed. "Delight has real rubies in her ears! Mom, can I get my ears pierced?"

Her mother came out of the kitchen, carrying a plate of sandwiches. "You can get your ears pierced when you are twelve and not a moment sooner. Besides, who could see your earrings under all that hair?"

Mrs. Wakefield appeared in the doorway to the dining room.

"Ladies," she said formally, making the girls giggle. "This way, please."

Carrying their stuffed animals, the girls followed Mrs. Wakefield.

"Ooooh!" Mindy said.

Amber gasped.

The dining room had been transformed into a Valentine fairyland. The round dining table was skirted in pink. A lace cloth covered the pink tablecloth like a dusting of snow. White candles glimmered in the silver candlesticks.

Near the window was a second, smaller table, draped in white. This was the party table for the girls' stuffed animals. Paper hearts told where each stuffed animal was to sit.

Amber ran over and put R.C. in his seat. Mindy found her stuffed penguin's place, and Delight propped Row-bear in the last chair.

"Look," Delight said. "Our places are marked with a cookie with our name on it." She picked up the pink-iced, heart-shaped "Delight" cookie and started to take a bite.

"Not yet," Amber said, remembering her job as hostess. "We have to pour the tea first."

Mrs. Cantrell brought in the teapot, which was filled with raspberry punch. Amber poured punch into three china cups.

The girls sipped "tea" and nibbled peanut butter and jelly sandwiches cut into heart shapes. The stuffed animals "ate" pink-iced cakes and stared at one another.

"Everything is so pretty," Mindy said.

Delight agreed. "It's just perfect, Amber."

Amber smiled happily. This was her first important party. She was glad everything was going well.

"More tea?" she asked Delight politely.

Delight held out her cup, her pinky finger curved elegantly. "Indubitably," she said, stumbling over the word.

The girls broke up.

"We should do this for every holiday," Mindy said. "What's after Valentine's Day?"

"Lincoln's Birthday," Amber said.

Mindy made a face. "I mean a fun holiday."

"St. Patrick's Day," Delight replied.

"There's Easter, too," said Amber. "We could have Easter eggs in little baskets—" She stopped.

"What is it?" asked Mindy.

She toyed with the paper Cupid who guarded her plate. "I was just thinking about Lisa and Carly. They wanted to come to my party, too. But I wanted it to be just us."

"They wouldn't have known if David hadn't fooled around with my invitation," Delight said. "Only a boy would mess things up."

"I don't know why we need boys at all," Amber said. "Why can't there just be girls?"

"Or a place where the boys could all go and leave us girls alone," Mindy suggested.

"A boy planet!" Delight said, laughing.

"I'd send Justin there on the first rocket," Amber declared.

"All the boys in our class are so icky," Mindy said.

"Not all of them," Delight said. "A couple aren't so bad."

Amber was surprised. She didn't think Delight liked boys. "Which ones aren't icky?" she pressed.

"I don't know *exactly*," Delight said, giggling. "I just don't think they're all terrible."

Amber eyed Delight over the rim of her teacup.

She wondered if David Jackson was one of the boys Delight thought wasn't so bad. Maybe the *only* boy.

When the party was over, Amber walked her guests to the door. "It's still snowing," she said.

"Maybe we won't have school tomorrow," Mindy said hopefully.

" 'Bye, Amber," Delight said. "I had a nice time."

"Me, too." Mindy ran through the snow to her house across the street.

Amber waved to her friends until they were gone. Turning to go back inside, she noticed footprints underneath the dining room window. They were too small to be Justin's. Who had been walking around their house?

Then she spied a bright red mitten lying in the snow, like a lone Valentine. She picked it up. Someone *had* been there, spying on her party!

Voices made her look up. Henry Hoffstedder and David Jackson came down the street, carrying snow saucers. David had one hand tucked in his pocket. On the other hand was a bright red mitten!

"Hey, David!" Amber called. "Come over here."

Leaving Henry on the corner, David walked up to Amber's door. "What do you want?"

She held up the mitten. "Lose this?"

"Yeah, that's mine." He took it from her. "Thanks."

"I know you were here," Amber said. "I saw your footprints. How come you were hanging around my house?"

David stared at the tips of his boots. "I just wanted to see your fancy party. Don't tell Henry. He'll laugh at me. Your party looked like fun."

"It was fun. We had cookies and punch and sandwiches."

David nodded. "I saw. You look nice," he added, somewhat embarrassed.

Amber felt a sudden warmth in her stomach, like the first swallow of homemade vegetable soup. He thought she looked nice in her white dress! David was paying attention to her the way he used to, before Delight came to their class. And he looked so cute, with one mitten on and one mitten off.

"Wait here," she said, dashing back inside the house. She came out a few seconds later with a pink-iced cookie. "Here. We have lots left over."

"Thanks," David said, taking the cookie. "See you in school tomorrow."

"Maybe we won't have school."

His face lit up. "Yeah! A snow day!" Then he said, "But tomorrow's Valentine's Day. I hope we go. Don't tell Henry I said that!"

"I won't," Amber promised.

She watched him head up the hill where Henry was waiting. She expected him to eat the cookie. Instead, he wrapped the cookie in the dropped red mitten and put it in his pocket.

Was he going to eat it later? Amber wondered. He

probably didn't want to share it with that greedy Henry.

But David was walking so dreamily up the hill, she thought he might be sick. Then Amber realized the truth.

David wasn't going to eat that cookie. He was going to keep it. Not because he was sick or because he didn't want to share it with Henry.

David was acting weird because he was in love.

Her on-again, off-again boyfriend was in love. With *her*!

FOUR

Got you!"

The snowball came from nowhere and smacked Amber on the arm.

After helping her mother clean up from the party, Amber had gone outside to build a snowman. It was still snowing, and at least five inches of fluffy snow lay on the ground. She could build a *big* snowman this time.

But she wasn't about to put up with flying snowballs.

"Justin!" she yelled. "You quit that!"

Her brother was standing by their next-door neighbor's garage. He had a snow shovel in his hand.

"It wasn't me!" he said. "I'm cleaning Mr. Murray's driveway."

Amber whirled and saw a familiar car at the curb.

Her father came out from behind a tree, laughing.

"Daddy!" she shrieked. "It was you!"

"Guilty," he admitted, picking her up in a bear hug.

Justin bounded across the yard. "Hey, Dad!"

It had been several weeks since they had last seen their father. Although Mr. Cantrell lived across the Potomac River in Maryland, he usually visited Amber and Justin on weekends. Often he took them back to his apartment in Maryland. They would eat in restaurants and go to the movies or to the shopping mall.

But last fall, when Amber began third grade, her father began visiting a lady in Philadelphia on weekends. Now Amber and Justin sometimes saw their father during the week, but seldom on weekends.

That was why she was so surprised to see him on this stormy Sunday afternoon.

"How come you're here?" Amber asked.

"I felt like building a snowman," her father replied, setting her down with a snowy plop. "So I came to see the two best snowman builders on Carriage Street." He pretended to scan the horizon. "Only I don't see them. I wonder where they are."

Amber giggled. "Daddy, you're so funny!"

While Justin and her father rolled a huge snowball for the snowman's body, Amber told him about her Valentine's Day tea party.

"It sounds terrific," her father remarked. "I wish I had been there."

"No, you don't," Justin said. "All those girls yakking about stuffed animals—"

"You don't know what we talked about," Amber said airily. "Boys don't know everything, do they, Daddy?"

Justin hooted. "Amber, what do you think *Dad* is?"

"Well, he's not a boy anymore." Amber patted the snowball into a firm, round shape. "At least he doesn't act dumb like boys do."

When the snowman was finished, Amber wound her muffler around its neck. Mr. Cantrell contributed his hat and Justin added the snow shovel. It was the best snowman in the world.

The snow had finally stopped falling. It was growing dark. Streetlights cast yellow pools upon the white lawns. Amber didn't want the day to end.

Suddenly her father flung himself backward, pulling Amber with him.

"Snow angels!" Justin cried, flinging himself down beside them.

They fanned their outstretched arms and legs and then got up carefully. In the snow were three angel-shaped impressions.

The front door opened. "Come on in for cocoa," Mrs. Cantrell called.

They went inside, stamping snow from their boots.

"I should be getting back," Mr. Cantrell said.

"Stay a little longer," Amber pleaded.

"All right." Her father took off his coat. Underneath he wore a tweed jacket. The lapel of his jacket sported a jaunty red carnation.

They all sat around the kitchen table and sipped mugs of steaming cocoa. Amber dunked her marshmallow and stared at her father. It seemed strange to see him in the kitchen again, sitting in his old chair. For a few seconds, it was almost as if he had never left.

"Where did you get the flower?" Mrs. Cantrell asked him. "A secret admirer?"

Mr. Cantrell looked down at the carnation and smiled. "Someone I met recently. Her name is Jennifer Donovan."

Amber's eyes grew wide. "Is Jennifer your new girlfriend?"

Justin nudged her with his elbow. "Be quiet. You aren't supposed to ask nosy questions."

"It's all right," their father said. "Yes, you can say Jennifer is a special friend. She works in my office. Maybe you and Justin can meet her sometime." He turned to Mrs. Cantrell. "How's business these days?"

Her parents talked about Mrs. Cantrell's shop for a while. Then Mr. Cantrell said he had to go.

After her father left, Amber decided to work on her Valentines for the school party tomorrow.

As she passed the kitchen, where her mother and Justin were clearing up, she overheard Justin say, "Sounds like Dad is really gone on this Jennifer."

"Yes," Mrs. Cantrell agreed. "That explains his giddiness today, driving all the way over here during a snowstorm to make a snowman with you kids."

"We made snow angels, too," Justin said. "He was acting like a kid Amber's age."

Amber leaned closer. Over the clink of spoons and mugs, she heard her mother sigh.

"Your father is obviously head over heels in love," she said. "And a whirlwind courtship, in my opinion, is not good for anybody."

Amber turned and went into her room. What was a whirlwind courtship? Was it anything like the cyclone in the Pecos Bill story? She pictured her father in a cowboy outfit, lassoing a whirlwind. Pecos Bill, she recalled, had an awful time trying to tame that cyclone.

Then she wondered if David Jackson was head over heels in love with her. He certainly looked weird after she gave him that cookie.

When her mother came in later to tell her it was bath time, Amber said, "Mom, did you have a boyfriend in third grade?"

"No, but I had a boyfriend in second grade."

"Who?"

"His name was Danny Blevins. He gave me a dime-store ring. We were terribly in love. I promised to marry him."

Amber sat up, fascinated. "What happened? How come you didn't marry him?"

Her mother smiled. "I decided he wasn't my type."

Was David her type? She liked him, some times more than others. But she didn't know if she loved him.

"How do you know if a boy is your type?" she asked.

"You have a long time before you have to worry about that," her mother said. "Now, hop in the tub."

Her mother was wrong. Amber didn't have a long time to worry. Tomorrow was Valentine's Day. She had less than twenty-four hours to decide if she was head over heels in love with David Jackson.

The Valentine's box sat on a table at the front of the room. Mrs. Sharp set up bottles of fruit juice around a plate of pink-iced cupcakes on her desk.

Students filed up and dropped batches of white or red envelopes into the slot on top of the Valentine's box.

The snow hadn't closed school, but school had started two hours late. Now the day was shorter and they had a lot to do.

First, they were having their class party. Afterward, they would go to a Valentine's Day assembly.

Amber felt a thrill of excitement. Anything could happen on Valentine's Day! Secret admirers would give their hearts . . . true loves would be revealed.

"Has everyone put their cards in the box?" Mrs. Sharp asked.

"Not me," Amber replied.

The surface of her desk was littered with small red envelopes. Those were the "penny" Valentines, as her mother called them, that Amber was sending to her classmates.

To one side were three large white envelopes. Those held the special Valentines that Amber had made for Mindy, Delight, and her teacher.

Two of the "penny" Valentines lay face-up on her desk. They had not yet been sealed into envelopes.

One showed a pair of green parrots in a silver cage. The cage was decorated with silver glitter. In hearts around the edge were the words "Let's be love birds." It was the prettiest card that came in the assortment.

The other card was funny. It showed a snake tied in a knot and said, "Coming or going, you're my Valentine."

Amber couldn't decide which card to give to David. He would like the snake Valentine, because he was crazy about snakes. But it wasn't a very special card.

She had considered making him a Valentine, but thought that would make her look too eager. He hadn't actually *said* he was in love with her. And she wasn't sure she was in love with him. Did a warm, vegetable-soup feeling in the stomach mean love?

"Amber," Mrs. Sharp reminded her. "The class is waiting."

"Yeah, Amber," said Henry. "Get a move on."

She decided quickly. She would give the lovebird card to David, and the snake card to Henry Hoffstedder. On the back of the lovebird Valentine she wrote, *Love Amber*. She signed the back of the snake Valentine simply, *From Amber*.

Hurriedly, she shoved the last two Valentines into their envelopes. She addressed one to David and one to Henry. Gathering the pile of envelopes, she ran to the front of the room and dropped her cards into the box.

"All right," Mrs. Sharp said. "Will the Valentine mail carriers come to the front, please?"

Lisa and Jonathan had already been chosen to hand out Valentines. While the class watched, Lisa emptied the Valentine box on the table. Then she and Jonathan grabbed handfuls of cards and walked up and down the aisles, delivering Valentines.

Mrs. Sharp passed out paper cups filled with candy hearts. The classroom became festive.

Lisa dropped a small white envelope on Amber's desk. Then Jonathan dropped two small red envelopes on her desk. Her first Valentines!

Amber crunched a "U-R Sweet" green heart and opened the cards.

"One from Eileen, one from Eric, and one from Carly," she reported to Mindy.

Mindy opened the large white envelope that Lisa had just delivered. It was Amber's Valentine.

"Oh, this is pretty," she said. "Thanks, Amber."

"Glad you like it." Amber surveyed the new pile of envelopes on her desk. They were all "penny"-sized. Surely David would have gotten her a big, store-bought Valentine card, like Justin had bought for the girl he liked.

She opened her cards, hopeful because Lisa and Jonathan were still scurrying up and down the aisles with more Valentines.

The party was in full swing. Amber drank fruit punch and munched her cupcake, still waiting for David's special envelope to appear on her desk.

At last Lisa and Jonathan returned to their own seats.

"That's it?" Amber asked Lisa. "That's all the Valentines?"

"The box is empty," Lisa told her.

But there were no special oversized envelopes on Amber's desk. Only small ones.

Amber opened her remaining cards. The first Valentine showed Garfield the cat riding a pony. "Pardner," it said, "let's be Valentines."

In very small letters on the back was printed *From David.*

From David! Not *Love David?*

Disappointment arrowed through Amber's heart. She studied the Valentine. It wasn't special at all. David could have sent a card just like it to Carly or Mindy or even Mrs. Sharp.

Clutching her ordinary Valentine, Amber looked across the room at David. Obviously she was wrong—he wasn't head over heels in love with her after all.

He was still opening cards, too. Had he opened hers yet? What would he think, getting a mushy Valentine with lovebirds on it?

"Has everyone finished eating?" Mrs. Sharp wanted to know. "Bring your trash to the front. We have to leave for the Valentine assembly in three minutes."

Dejected, Amber scooped her Valentines into the cubby under her desk. Nothing special had happened on this day after all.

Then Henry Hoffstedder cried, "Yuck! Look what I got!" He held the lovebird Valentine between two fingers, as if it had germs.

Amber gasped.

That was David's Valentine! How had Henry

gotten David's Valentine?

Then it hit her. She must have put the lovebird Valentine in *Henry's* envelope!

"I'll never be *your* lovebird, Amber Cantrell," Henry said with disgust. "I'll fly south first!"

The worst had happened. Now that awful Henry Hoffstedder thought she was in love with *him*!

Chapter

FIVE

Did you see this gooey Valentine Amber sent me?" Henry complained loudly to David. "I bet it's got cooties!"

Students near Henry turned to look at him. He pretended to brush invisible bugs off the card.

"Amber's cooties are all over me!" he cried, encouraged by his audience's laughter.

"Henry Hoffstedder!" Mrs. Sharp rapped on her desk. "Did I tell you to talk? We are supposed to be getting in line for the assembly, not entertaining our neighbors."

Amber's face burned with humiliation. Now everyone in class knew that Henry Hoffstedder had received a gooey Valentine from Amber Cantrell. And she didn't even mean to send it to him!

They lined up at the door.

Amber stood behind Mindy and Delight. Delight was still opening her Valentines.

Peering over Delight's shoulder, Amber watched her friend take out a card with Garfield the cat wearing a fireman's helmet. She tried to see what was written on the back, but Delight quickly slipped the card back into the envelope.

Amber wondered if the Valentine was from David. He had sent her a Garfield card, too.

Lots of kids sent Garfield Valentines, she decided. Delight's card could have been sent by anyone in the class.

Just then, David asked Jonathan to trade places with him in line. Now he was standing right behind Amber.

"I liked your Valentine," he said to her. "You don't mind if I hang it on Titus's cage, do you? He'll like it, too."

Titus was David's pet garter snake. Amber wasn't fond of snakes, but she didn't have anything against hanging her Valentine on a snake's cage.

"No, I don't care," she said. "Maybe Titus will learn to tie himself in a knot like the snake on the card."

David broke up. "That's funny! You're always telling jokes, Amber. You're the funniest girl in third grade."

"You really think so?" Amber's spirits lifted.

David seemed to be paying her a lot of attention today.

He lowered his voice. "Did you like my card?"

"Your Valentine? Yeah. It's cute."

"I tried to find one with a raccoon on it," he said. "You know, like R.C. But I couldn't."

Amber couldn't believe her ears. He had tried to find a special Valentine for her!

"Oh, that's okay," she said. "I liked your Valentine a lot. I'll show it to R.C. when I get home. He'll like it, too."

David scuffed his sneaker against the floor. "Henry really liked the card you gave him."

Amber's eyes flashed. "He wasn't supposed to get that card. It was a mistake. I wouldn't be Henry Hoffstedder's Valentine in a million years!"

"Really?" David smiled, as if Amber had given him a present. "Guess what?"

"What?"

"I still have that cookie you gave me. I'm saving it."

Amber didn't have to ask why. Her heart was singing. She'd been right all along. David was really in love with her!

Just then Henry Hoffstedder pushed his way between Amber and David.

"Better watch out," he warned David. "Amber will probably kiss you or something gross like that."

David grinned at Amber over Henry's shoulder. He looked as if he wouldn't mind being kissed.

Henry accidentally-on-purpose bumped into Amber. "Ewww! Amber touched me! Cootie alert! Cootie alert!"

Henry's remarks didn't bother Amber anymore. She was so happy. Her on-again, off-again boyfriend really loved her. Suddenly the world was wonderful. No one—not even icky Henry—could make her feel bad.

"Henry Hoffstedder," she said, putting him firmly in his place. "Act your age, not your hat size."

At home, Amber displayed all her Valentines on the bookshelves in the living room. Her mother came in to admire them.

"What a nice collection, Amber. You received some terrific cards."

"This one is from David Jackson." Amber proudly pointed to the Garfield card that occupied a shelf of its own. "He picked it out especially for me. Isn't it cute?"

Her mother smiled at her. "Are you and David special friends?"

Amber moved Mrs. Sharp's card closer to Mindy's. "I think so," she said, not looking at her mother.

She felt like she did whenever she rode the Ferris wheel at the carnival, happy and excited and scared, with a little upset stomach thrown in for good measure. She guessed it was love.

"Am-ber's got a boy-friend!" Justin sang from the doorway.

Amber whirled on her brother. "Mom! Tell him to be quiet!"

"Justin," Mrs. Cantrell said. "You will not make fun of your sister. This is what Valentine's Day is for, to find out if someone thinks you're special. Speaking of which, did *you* get any Valentines?"

"Nobody would send Justin a Valentine," Amber couldn't resist saying. "Unless they were crazy."

"They'd have to be blind to send *you* one!" Justin fired back.

"Kids!" Mrs. Cantrell's tone ended the argument. "You didn't answer my question, Justin. Did you get any Valentines?"

"Maybe," he said evasively. He glanced at Amber's collection on the bookshelves. "But I'm not putting it out for everybody to see!" With that, he slammed into his room.

Mrs. Cantrell grinned at Amber. "He got a Valentine!"

"Jus-tin has a girl-friend!" Amber chanted.

Later, when she was in bed, Amber realized her mother had not received a special card. Amber had given her mother a card, and so had Justin. But that was all.

She stared at David's card, which was now propped against the lamp on her night table. She was planning to keep it there forever and ever, so she could see it first thing in the morning and last thing at night.

She felt bad that her mother didn't have a card to prop up against *her* night-table lamp.

Throwing back the covers, Amber padded barefoot down the hall to the living room, where her mother was working on papers from her shop. She flung her arms around her mother.

"What's all this?" Mrs. Cantrell asked, laughing. "You're supposed to be in bed."

"I just wanted to say Happy Valentine's Day." She gave her mother another squeeze, then hopped back down the hall to her warm, rumpled bed.

"Amber, your father will be here any minute," Mrs. Cantrell said. "Are you ready?"

"Yes," she replied, grabbing her purse off the doorknob.

It was Sunday. Mr. Cantrell was taking Amber and Justin to brunch. They were going to meet Jennifer, Mr. Cantrell's new lady friend, for the first time.

Amber had dressed carefully for the event. She wore the new red-and-black Scottie dog dress she had received for Christmas. Her long hair was held back by red Scottie barrettes. Even her plastic purse had a Scottie on the pocket. She thought she looked as grown-up as Delight Wakefield.

Justin was waiting on the sofa. He looked at Amber in her Scottie splendor and said rudely, "Where's the dog show?"

"Mom! Justin's picking on me again!"

"Justin, that remark was uncalled for. Apologize to your sister."

"Sorry," he told Amber grudgingly.

Mrs. Cantrell frowned at him. "What's wrong with you today, Justin? You're grumpier than a groundhog."

"I don't like brunch," he replied. "I like to go out for breakfast or for lunch. But I don't like the food all mixed up."

"I love brunch," Amber said, smoothing her skirt. "I'm going to have waffles and sausage and those little pink cakes—"

"Nobody cares what you're going to eat!" Her brother's scowl grew deeper.

Mrs. Cantrell sat down beside him. "Did something happen at school this week? Between you and a girl, perhaps?"

"I gave her a Valentine," he blurted. "It cost me two whole dollars. And she gave me a card, too. All week I waited for her at her locker and we talked, and I thought she liked me. But then I found out she's going to the dance Friday with Kevin Hartley. And he didn't even give her a Valentine!"

Amber stared at Justin. He looked so miserable, she didn't even mind his nasty remark about her Scottie dog outfit.

Mrs. Cantrell patted Justin's knee. "Maybe your friend had already agreed to go to the dance with this other boy before Valentine's Day. Maybe she had been waiting for *you* to ask her, and this Kevin asked her first."

Justin looked up hopefully. "You think so? I don't think she likes him as much as she likes me."

"Give her a chance." Mrs. Cantrell glanced out the window. "Your father's here. Have a good time, you two."

They ran out and jumped into the car.

"Where's Jennifer?" Amber asked, buckling her seat belt.

"She's meeting us at the restaurant," Mr. Cantrell replied. He pushed the button on the cassette player.

Music blasted from the car speakers. Justin began tapping his foot in time to the beat.

Amber frowned. "That sounds like the music Justin listens to. You don't usually play that kind of stuff, Daddy. You always said it isn't good like the music from your day."

"I like the new music, too," her father said. "Jennifer got me this tape for Valentine's Day."

At the restaurant, Mr. Cantrell asked for a table for four. "Jennifer will be here any minute," he said as they sat down. "A soda for you, Justin? Amber, what would you like to drink?"

Amber ordered her favorite drink, a Shirley Temple. She would give the little paper parasol to R.C.

The drinks came, but Jennifer didn't. Amber was getting hungry. She was about to complain when she saw her father's face light up.

"Here she is!" he said, springing out of his chair.

Beside her, Justin exclaimed softly, "Wow!" Amber looked toward the door.

Her father's new lady friend was very pretty and very young. She had shoulder-length blonde hair and blue eyes. She wore a lot more makeup than Amber's mother did. Her skirt was also a lot shorter than the ones Amber's mother wore.

Mr. Cantrell rushed forward to pull out Jennifer's chair. Amber had never seen him move so fast.

"Amber, Justin, this is Jennifer Donovan," he said proudly. "Jennifer, these are my children, Amber and Justin."

"Hi, everybody," Jennifer chirped. "Sorry I'm late. Cupid got lost and I couldn't find him. You'll never guess where he was hiding! Under the washing machine!"

Amber stared at her, confused. "Who's Cupid?" she asked.

Jennifer laughed. "My kitten! Your father gave me the sweetest little white kitten for Valentine's Day."

A kitten for Valentine's Day! Amber was impressed. She would love to have a present like that.

She looked over at Justin. He was gaping at Jennifer Donovan as if she were an alien from Mars. Her father was smiling at Jennifer, who was still chattering about her kitten.

"Can we eat?" Amber asked. "I'm hungry."

"Of course we can eat," her father said. He let Amber lead the way to the buffet line.

"I love your dress," Jennifer said to Amber. "It's so cute. Red is your color."

"Thanks. I like your skirt, too." Amber felt very grown-up, talking to her father's girlfriend about clothes.

She loaded her plate with sausage and waffles and whipped cream. She would come back later for the pink cakes.

Busy staring at Jennifer, Justin absently filled his plate with bacon and hash browns. Amber watched in amazement as he poured warm syrup over his potatoes.

"You don't put syrup on potatoes," she said, annoyed. "What's the matter with you? You act like you've never seen a girl before."

"Not like her."

Amber couldn't see what was so special about Jennifer. She was pretty and nice, but so was Amber's mother.

When they all sat back down, Amber noticed Jennifer had only fruit and cottage cheese on her plate.

"You ought to try a waffle," she said. "They're really yummy. You can get whipped cream *and* syrup on it."

Jennifer laughed. "If I did that, I'd end up looking like a cow in no time. Be glad you can eat anything you want, Amber."

"My mother eats anything she wants," Amber said. "And she doesn't look like a cow."

There was a small silence. Amber wondered if she had made a mistake, mentioning her mother in front of her father's new friend. She had never been out with her father and his girlfriend before. She didn't know what she was supposed to say or not say.

"Then your mother is very lucky," Jennifer said lightly. "The waffle *does* look yummy, but I'll stick to fruit."

"Jennifer is into fitness," Mr. Cantrell told Amber and Justin. "How often do you go to an exercise class?"

"Well, I go to aerobics four times a week, and then twice a week I lift weights."

Justin's tone was filled with admiration. "You lift weights?"

"Jennifer is very strong," Mr. Cantrell said proudly.

Amber felt a little sick. Maybe she had put too much whipped cream on her waffle. Then she realized that her father had barely touched the food on his plate. He hadn't stopped looking at Jennifer the whole time.

"Daddy, you're not eating," she said.

"I'm not really hungry," he replied.

Amber knew this was not good. Whenever she wasn't hungry, her mother felt her forehead to see if she had a temperature. Her father didn't look as if he had a temperature, but he didn't seem like himself either.

It must be the whirlwind courtship, she decided. Her mother was right. A whirlwind courtship was not good for him.

Amber didn't want her father to become ill. There was only one thing to do. She would have to rescue him.

SIX

Ways to be Famous

1. *boat race*
2. *plant seeds*
3. *giant blue raccoon*

Amber stared at the list she had been working on since reading period.

Mrs. Sharp had read more legends in class today. One was about Johnny Appleseed, who planted apple seeds all over the country. Johnny Appleseed was a real person. He was not a giant like Paul Bunyan. But he looked odd, with a tin saucepan on his head and no shoes.

After reading, Mrs. Sharp let the class work on their own legends. Amber worked on her own project instead of the assignment.

Even with all the love problems around her

house—hers, Justin's, her father's—she had not given up the idea of becoming a Third Grade Legend. She wanted to leave her mark like "FWR," who had once sat in her desk. She wanted people to talk about her for years to come.

Yet if she aimed to be a Third Grade Legend, she would have to do something legendary. Something that would make her unforgettable. "Amber Gillian Cantrell?" people would say. "Yes, I've heard of her. She was the most famous third-grader in our school."

She studied her list, chewing the end of her pencil. *Boat race,* the first item said. Mike Fink had won a steamboat race on the mighty Mississippi River and he had become a legend. If it worked for Mike Fink, it ought to work for Amber Cantrell.

But where would she find a river? The nearest body of water was Little Rocky Run, the stream that divided Amber's neighborhood from the bigger, newer houses of Mockingbird Ridge. Little Rocky Run was hardly a mighty river. Amber didn't know how to build a boat anyway, so she crossed number one off her list.

She went on to number two—*plant seeds*. She could do that. She didn't like apples that much. Peaches were better. Maybe she could plant peach seeds all over her neighborhood, the way Johnny Appleseed had planted apple seeds.

She pictured herself walking barefoot up and down Carriage Street, her mother's saucepan on her head. People would laugh at her! She crossed number two off her list.

Number three read *giant blue raccoon*. Paul Bunyan was famous because he had tamed the giant blue ox Babe. Amber didn't have an ox. All she had was R.C., her stuffed raccoon.

She could paint R.C. blue, though she didn't know how to make him bigger. Her raccoon was just the right size to hug, but he wasn't a giant.

Sadly, she crossed number three off her list. None of those things would work. She would have to think of another way to be a Third Grade Legend.

"Amber." Mindy was tapping on her desk.

"What?"

"I've been talking to you for five minutes. It's time for lunch. Don't you want to eat?"

Amber hadn't noticed the others around her leaving their seats, pulling lunch sacks from their cubbies.

"You must be finished with your legend," Mindy remarked as Amber put away her notebook.

"I haven't even started."

"What were you working on then?" Mindy asked.

"Something." Usually Amber loved to talk about her ideas, but she wanted to keep this one to herself. The purple "FWR '79" strip under her desk was a secret. Anyway, folk heroes didn't go around telling people they were trying to be a legend.

Delight met them at the door and they walked to the cafeteria together. Many students headed for the serving line, but Amber led her friends to an empty table.

"What are they having today?" Delight asked, wrinkling her nose. "It smells awful."

"Probably fried toenails." Amber opened her lunch sack. "I hope everybody likes tortilla chips. I got the round kind."

Once a week, Amber, Mindy, and Delight had Share Day for lunch. Instead of bringing individual lunches, each would bring one thing for the rest to share. This week it was Delight's turn to bring the sandwiches. Amber brought the juice boxes and "crunchies," as she called them. Mindy brought brownies.

Delight passed around tuna sandwiches. "Amber, Henry Hoffstedder keeps saying you're in love with him. You ought to hear him! I tell him to be quiet, but he just goes on."

"I am *not* in love with Henry Hoffstedder," Amber stated.

"Nobody believes him," Mindy said, her mouth full. "Who could be in love with Henry?"

"It's because I accidentally sent him the wrong Valentine," Amber explained. "But it turned out okay. I mean, the one who was supposed to get the Valentine didn't mind."

Delight's eyes grew round. "Amber, you like somebody! Who is it?"

Amber glanced at David, who was sitting at the next table.

"Not David Jackson?" Mindy guessed.

Amber fumbled with her straw wrapper.

"It *is* David Jackson!" Mindy squealed. "You love David!"

"Shhhh!" Amber was afraid he would hear.

"Does he like you back?" Delight asked. She seemed very interested in Amber's answer.

"He was the one who started it," Amber said. "I gave him a cookie and he saved it. And then he tried to find a raccoon Valentine to give me, but he gave me a Garfield one instead." She paused to drink some juice. "He lets me get ahead of him in line at the water fountain. And he doesn't kick me in gym anymore."

"Gee, he acts the same way to me," Delight said. "I kind of thought David liked me."

"Well, he sent *me* a special Valentine," Amber said. This was one time when she had something Delight didn't have.

"I got a Garfield Valentine from David, too," Delight said.

"Really?" Amber felt a stab of jealousy. So that card *was* from David. "Did it say anything special on the back? Because mine did."

"What did he write?" Delight wanted to know.

"Never mind," Amber replied mysteriously.

David hadn't written anything special on the back of her Valentine, but his name was printed very neatly. Only a boy who really liked a girl would sign his name with such care.

Still, Amber wasn't so sure about David's feelings now. If he liked her, why had David given Delight a Garfield card, too? Who did he like best?

"I guess it *is* true love," Delight said with a sigh.

Amber picked thoughtfully at her sandwich. "I think it's in the air. Justin has a girlfriend, sort of, and even my dad is acting weird over this lady from his office."

"I was in my cousin's wedding last summer," Mindy said. "I heard her say that all her friends were getting married at the same time. It's like a fever or something."

"I can't wait to get married so I can wear a pretty dress and carry flowers," said Amber.

"Me, too," Delight agreed.

"I can wait," Mindy said. "Boys are dumb."

As if to prove her point, Henry Hoffstedder walked by with his lunch trash. He pretended to trip and nearly dumped his tray onto Amber's head.

"Definitely weird," Amber said. "I wonder why we have boys in this world. We certainly don't need them."

After lunch, they had a math test.

"That's another thing we don't need in this world," Amber said to Mindy. "Math tests."

Before Mrs. Sharp passed out the papers, she declared a brief Errand Time.

"Get that drink of water now," she said. "And sharpen your pencils. I want you to be prepared for this test."

Amber looked at her pencil. She had sharpened it twice that day already. It wasn't really dull. But she could think better if the point of her pencil was extra-sharp.

She got in the line at the pencil sharpener. David Jackson saw her and left his seat to stand in line behind her.

Amber's heart pounded. She knew David didn't need to sharpen his pencil. He just wanted to stand next to her.

"Amber, I have to tell you something," he whispered.

"What?" she whispered back. It was her turn at the pencil sharpener. She stuck her pencil in the hole and turned the crank very slowly.

"I . . . uh . . . you know I like you, Amber," he stammered. "A lot. And I think you like me, too. Right?"

"Yes, I like you." Actually, the warm-vegetable-soup feeling she had for David was stronger than like. But she didn't want to tell David she loved him until he said it first.

"Well . . . uh . . . I think . . . we ought to . . . will you marry me?"

Amber kept turning the crank on the pencil

sharpener. She was stunned. David Jackson had actually proposed to her! That meant he liked her more than anyone in the classroom! More than Delight!

"Can you hurry with your answer?" he said, fidgeting. "Mrs. Sharp is passing out the test."

Amber replied without hesitation. "Yes, I will marry you."

"Good." David turned to go back to his seat.

"Wait! What about a ring?"

He stopped. "A what?"

"A ring," she repeated. "You have to give me an engagement ring."

He thought about this for a second. Amber was worried he might change his mind.

"Okay," he said finally. "I'll get you a ring."

When Amber returned to her seat, she was grinning.

"What happened?" Mindy asked immediately. "I saw David ask you something. What did he want?"

Amber saw that Mrs. Sharp was passing out test papers on the far side of the room.

"He asked me to marry him!" Amber replied. "He's going to give me a ring! I'm engaged!"

"I thought you didn't like boys," Mindy said. "You said boys are weird. How can you get engaged to one?"

"Boys *are* weird," Amber explained. "But not all of them. David's okay."

He was more than okay. He was *wonderful*.

"Well." Mindy didn't sound very pleased. "I guess you know what you're doing. When are you getting married?"

"I don't know. He just asked me."

"You have to set a date," Mindy advised.

Amber still couldn't believe she was engaged. Now she had to set a wedding date! She wondered if third-graders were allowed to get married. Where would she and David live? At his house or hers? She hoped they would live at her house—she didn't want to leave her room after her mother had fixed it up.

Mrs. Sharp placed a test paper on her desk. Amber looked at the first problem. How could she possibly think about math problems at a time like this? She wondered if the teacher would excuse her because she had just gotten engaged.

Later, during art period, Amber broke the news to Delight.

Delight's face fell. "Are you sure David asked you to marry him? You didn't hear wrong?"

"I heard him very clearly," Amber said. "He said he was madly in love with me and he wanted to marry me more than anything."

Of course, David hadn't said any of those things, but Amber was sure he *would* have if he had thought of them. She was glad to see Delight was not happy over the news. Now Delight knew who David liked best!

"I want to wear a long, white dress and carry

roses," Amber said. "And wear a veil." She put a sheet of white construction paper on her head and hummed "Here Comes the Bride."

Delight fashioned a ring from a strip of paper. She placed it on Amber's finger.

"I now pronounce you husband and wife," Mindy intoned. The girls cracked up.

Delight leaned toward Amber. "There goes David to get more supplies. Why don't you tell him you want to set the date?"

"I don't know." Amber twisted the paper ring on her finger. She had just been asked. She didn't want to seem too pushy.

"You can't wait for the boy," Mindy said with authority. "My cousin said so and she ought to know about these things. You have to tell them what you want."

"Okay." Amber pushed back her chair and marched up to the supply cabinet. "David," she said to him. "When are we getting married?"

He looked up from the bin of markers he was rooting through. "I don't know," he replied absently. "I haven't really thought about it. When do you want to get married?"

"Soon," Amber said. "How about tomorrow?"

"That's too soon," he said quickly. "I mean, I haven't even got your ring yet. Don't you want to wear it a few days before we get married?"

That sounded reasonable to her. "Okay," she said. "You get me the ring first. You're going to bring me one tomorrow, right?"

He located the marker he'd been looking for. "Okay."

Feeling reassured, Amber went back to her seat and reported to Mindy and Delight.

Delight nodded. "You should be engaged a while. That way you can show off your ring."

"But not too long," cautioned Mindy. "My aunt said a long engagement is bad luck."

Now Amber was worried. "How long is too long?"

"I don't know. Maybe a month."

"I'll be married before then," Amber said confidently. "David is crazy about me. He won't want to wait."

Delight sighed with envy. "I wish I had a boyfriend. You're so lucky, Amber Cantrell. I bet you're the first person in our class to get married. Maybe even in the whole school."

Amber smiled. She just thought of something. Now she wouldn't have to figure out how to become a Third Grade Legend. Her problem was solved.

For years to come, people would remember her as the first girl in Virginia Run Elementary to get married.

Chapter
SEVEN

Here it is!" Amber told R.C. triumphantly. "It would be way at the bottom."

She was in her mother's room, leaning into an open cedar chest. On the rug around her lay folded quilts and old tablecloths.

Her mother stored her best antique quilts and linens in the chest. Amber knew her mother wouldn't sell these things because she liked them so well.

Reaching deep into the chest, she pulled out a muslin-wrapped bundle.

"This is very special," she told R.C. The stuffed raccoon, as always, listened to every word she said. "It was made by a lady a long time ago. It's very old."

Amber unwrapped the muslin to reveal a bedspread crocheted in ivory lace.

Leaving the quilts scattered on the rug, she

gathered up R.C. and the crocheted coverlet and went into her room.

In front of her mirror, she draped the bedspread around her shoulders. Holding the front closed with one hand, she studied her reflection.

She looked pretty. R.C. stared approvingly from the dresser. Yes, the bedspread would make a fine wedding dress.

Having David Jackson ask her to marry him was just about the neatest thing that had happened to her all year. It was even neater than taking gymnastics lessons. She felt so special, she spun in front of the mirror.

Just then her door opened. Her brother walked in.

"You're supposed to knock!" Amber said, startled.

"How many times do you knock on my door?" he returned. "Dad called a few minutes ago. I yelled, but you never answered."

"I was . . . busy," she said, afraid to admit she was rummaging in their mother's room. "How come he called?"

"He wanted to invite us to dinner with him and Jennifer. This weekend."

"I wish I had talked to him. Why didn't you yell louder for me?"

Justin leaned against the door and crossed his arms. "You know, Amber, sometimes I like to talk to Dad myself."

"What did you two talk about?" she asked.

"Man stuff."

She sputtered with laughter. "You?"

"Yes, me!" He lifted his chin. "In case you haven't noticed, I have serious problems."

"Mom said your face would clear up when you got older."

He flushed. "That's not what Dad and I talked about! You wouldn't understand. You're just a little kid."

"I'm not that little. I'm almost the tallest girl in my class." Curious about her brother's problem, she prompted, "Tell me what you said to Dad. I won't make fun."

"There's this girl at school," he began. "I gave her a Valentine and she gave me one, but she went to the dance with Kevin Hartley. And yet she tells me she likes me better."

"So? You knew she was going to the dance with this other guy."

"We're having another dance next Friday. I asked her to go with me," Justin went on. "She told me she has to visit her grandmother that night. That's a trick girls use when they don't want to say yes or no, in case somebody else asks them."

Amber plucked at the coverlet. "Maybe she really does have to go see her grandmother."

"That's what Dad said. I don't know." He sighed. "I think girls play games. They lay little traps for guys to walk into. You can't trust them."

"You can, too!" Amber said. "You can trust girls a lot more than boys!"

"Girls are weird."

"Boys are weirder!"

Suddenly Justin noticed the coverlet wrapped around her. "What have you got on? It looks like one of Mom's fancy old bedspreads."

"It is. I borrowed it," she replied.

He gave her a skeptical glance. "Without telling Mom, I bet. Why, may I ask, are you wearing a bedspread?"

Amber drew herself up. "I'm getting married. This is my wedding dress."

Now it was Justin's turn to sputter with laughter. "Getting married! Now I've heard everything!"

"It's true!" Amber said. "David Jackson asked me to marry him."

"Where?"

"At the pencil sharpener."

He laughed again. "I mean, where are you getting married? Is it going to be a church wedding? Or are you going to get married at a fancy hotel? Have you set a date?"

Flustered, Amber took off the bedspread. She never realized there were so many details to getting married. Set a date, find a place. All she thought she had to do was wear a long dress and carry flowers.

"I don't know where we're getting married," she

said. "Or when. He only asked me today. even have my engagement ring yet."

Her brother's voice took on a teasing tone. thought you didn't like boys. You said you can't trust them. You think they're weird."

"They are," Amber said. "Except for David. He's the only boy I'd ever marry."

"He's the only one who asked, you mean."

Furious, she flapped the bedspread at him. "At least somebody asked me! Nobody will ever ask you, Justin Cantrell."

"Don't worry. I'm not going to let some girl trap *me*." Before leaving, he added bossily, "And you better not let Mom catch you dragging her bedspread on the floor."

Amber stuck out her tongue. It wasn't much, but it was all she could do to a closed door.

Listening to him stomp down the hall, Amber decided she wouldn't stay mad at her brother. Not this time. Justin was miserable over that girl he liked. Love made people do strange things. Look at how silly her father acted since he started going with Jennifer. It was too bad Justin wasn't as happy as she was.

Spinning once more before the mirror, Amber flung out the bedspread like a flag. Love was grand!

"My cousin got her ring in a restaurant," Mindy told Amber.

They were on the bus on their way to school. Amber had hardly slept the night before, thinking about the engagement ring David was going to give her today.

"Her boyfriend dropped it in her water glass when she wasn't looking," Mindy went on. "When she went to drink, the ring was at the bottom of her glass!"

"It's a wonder she didn't swallow it," Amber said. She hoped David wouldn't try anything like that. She would hate to find her ring at the bottom of her milk carton, all milky and yucky.

"I heard about this girl who got a diamond ring on the end of a balloon," said Delight. "Do you suppose David will get you a diamond?"

"Diamonds are expensive," Amber said. "But he promised to get me something nice." He hadn't, but Amber was enjoying her role as bride-to-be.

Delight looked envious. "I really wish I had a boyfriend," she said wistfully. "I think David Jackson is the cutest boy in the class."

"Yes, he is," Amber agreed.

"I always thought he liked me," Delight went on. "He's really nice to me. And he gave me a neat Valentine."

"Well, he likes *me* best," Amber said smugly. Delight would have to find her own boyfriend. David was taken. He was Amber's own true love.

As the bus drew closer to the school, Amber grew more anxious about her ring.

The instant the bus stopped, she jumped down the steps and ran into the building. She didn't even wait for Mindy and Delight.

Dashing into Room Six, she found her own true love leafing through a book about reptiles.

"Did you bring it?" she asked, hanging breathlessly over David's desk.

He looked up. "Oh, hi, Amber. Did I bring what?"

"My ring!" How could he forget? He had only asked her to marry him the day before.

"Oh, that. Yeah, I brought it."

David scanned the room. Henry Hoffstedder was bugging Carly. The other kids were talking. Satisfied no one was looking, he reached into his pocket and pulled out an object concealed in his fist.

Amber presented her left hand, sticking out the fourth finger.

He looked horrified. "You don't expect me to put it on your hand, do you? Right in front of everybody?"

"I thought we'd practice for when we really get married."

David kept his fist closed. Obviously he didn't want to practice. With a sigh, Amber opened her palm flat. He dropped something into it.

It was not a diamond ring. In fact, the ring was made of pink plastic, with a Barbie doll emblem in the center.

Amber tried to put the Barbie ring on her finger. It was too small for the fourth finger. She put it on her pinky instead. It pinched only a little.

"It's very pretty," she said, trying to hide her disappointment.

"It's my little sister's," David told her. "She let me have it, but I have to take her turn on dish night for a week."

"Really?" Amber's disappointment changed to gratitude. Her true love would suffer doing dishes just to get her an engagement ring. "Thanks a lot. I love it."

"I'm glad." He added nervously, "Don't flash it around too much."

"Why not? We're getting married, aren't we?" Amber couldn't wait to show off her new ring.

"Yeah, but—"

Just then Mrs. Sharp called the class to order. Amber hurried to her seat.

For the rest of the morning, the teacher kept the class busy. There was no opportunity for Amber to show off her ring until lunchtime.

On the way down to the cafeteria, Amber showed the ring to Mindy.

Mindy made a face. "It's a Barbie ring. Not a diamond."

"I never said David would get me a diamond," Amber said testily. "He promised to do the dishes five whole nights just to get this ring."

"I wonder what's for lunch today?" Mindy said.

Amber had hoped her best friend would jump and squeal. Maybe Delight would act more enthusiastic.

But where *was* Delight? She wasn't with the rest of the class. In fact, neither was David Jackson.

Amber frowned. Why weren't her second-best friend and her fiancé in line? Did Mrs. Sharp make them stay behind for some reason?

As the students reached the cafeteria door, Amber saw Delight rushing up.

"Look at my ring!" Amber cried, holding up her hand.

"Look at *my* ring!" Delight said at the same time.

Amber stared. Delight wore a blue plastic ring crammed on the little finger of her left hand.

"Where did you get that?" she demanded.

"From David Jackson. He asked me to marry him."

"How can he ask you?" Amber shrieked. "He asked *me*!"

Delight looked at Amber's pink Barbie ring. "David told me you two weren't getting married after all. He said he wanted to marry me instead."

"I don't believe it!" Angry tears stung her eyes. "You double-crossed me, Delight Wakefield!"

"I didn't!"

"You're jealous because I have a boyfriend and you don't," Amber said. "You're trying to take him away from me!"

"I'm not!" Delight protested. "David came up and just gave me the ring. I didn't make him do it!"

"Yes, you did! I'm never speaking to you again!"

Just then David Jackson walked past with Henry Hoffstedder. Amber started to tug the pink ring off her finger. She wanted to throw it at David and let him know what she thought of him. But the ring was stuck.

"Amber," Delight was saying. "I thought you and David had a fight."

"You've always liked David," Amber accused. "You say so all the time. You just want my boyfriend!"

"I don't! I mean, I thought he was *my* boyfriend today." Delight slipped the blue ring off her finger. "Do you want me to give my ring back to him?"

Amber glared at her. How could Delight steal her boyfriend? Maybe she was one of those girls Justin talked about, the kind that trapped boys. That was it. Delight Wakefield somehow trapped David into proposing to her.

Then she looked over at David. His blond hair stuck up in a cowlick. He really *was* the cutest boy in class. She wouldn't let that scheming Delight Wakefield take him away from her.

Delight was no longer her second-best friend. She was Amber's rival.

"Keep your ring," Amber said huffily to Delight. "But keep your sticky hands off my boyfriend."

Her head held high, she marched into the cafeteria.

On the bus that afternoon, Amber made a big show of sitting far away from Delight Wakefield.

Delight was sitting alone in a seat near the front. When Amber boarded the bus, she pretended not to see Delight.

"Let's go to the back, Mindy," she said haughtily. "I don't like it up here."

Delight glanced in Amber's direction, but didn't speak. She sat with her hand posed so that everyone could see her ring.

Amber swept past Delight's seat. Mindy followed her to an empty seat at the rear and slid in beside her.

"Honestly, Amber," she said. "I thought you weren't going fight with Delight anymore."

"I'm not jealous of her this time," Amber said.

"I'm just plain mad. She's trying to steal my boyfriend!"

"I don't think it's Delight's fault David Jackson gave her a ring, too."

"Yes, it is," Amber insisted. "She tricked him somehow. She wants him for herself. Well, she can't have him. He's mine!"

Mindy shook her head. "All this trouble over a boy."

"Not just any boy," Amber said. "He's my own true love."

At home, Amber asked her mother if another girl had ever tried to steal her boyfriend.

"Not exactly," Mrs. Cantrell replied, as she cleaned the counter. "But one time my best friend and I liked the same boy. He couldn't make up his mind which one of us he liked the best."

Amber hoisted herself up on the kitchen stool. "What did you do? Did you and your friend fight?"

"Well, we both tried to impress him so he would choose. We were mad at each other for a while. Then we decided the whole thing was dumb. He wasn't worth breaking up our friendship over." Mrs. Cantrell finished wiping the counter and looked at Amber. "Are you having boyfriend troubles?"

"No. Yes. Sort of." Amber felt embarrassed to admit that her own true love had given an engagement ring to another girl. She sighed. "This love stuff is kind of confusing, isn't it?"

Her mother put her arm around Amber's shoulder. "Love is usually confusing," she said gently. "Sometimes you get hurt. But as a wise person once said, 'it's better to have loved and lost than never to have loved at all.'"

Amber had already made up her mind that *she* would be the one to win. The only problem was, she didn't want to lose her second-best friend either.

As soon as Amber saw her father, she knew his whirlwind courtship was making him worse.

It was Saturday night. Amber and Justin were going to dinner with their father and Jennifer.

"We have reservations at seven," Mr. Cantrell reminded them when he came to the door.

"I'm ready." Justin grabbed his jacket off the chair.

"Jennifer says this place is hard to get into." Mr. Cantrell stood in the doorway with his hands in his pockets. "We're lucky to get a table on a Saturday night."

Amber stared at her father. He was wearing jeans with holes in the knees, like Justin's friends were wearing. He had on a new jean jacket that fit stiffly across his shoulders. His hair was no longer parted on the side, but combed straight back.

He doesn't look like Daddy, she thought.

Mrs. Cantrell came to see them off. "Amber, put

your coat on. John, you're looking very well these days."

"No, he isn't. He looks—" Amber began, but her mother nudged her.

"I'll have them back by nine-thirty," Mr. Cantrell promised Mrs. Cantrell. He ushered Justin and Amber out the door.

Jennifer was waiting in the front seat of Mr. Cantrell's car. As Amber and Justin climbed into the backseat, she twisted around to greet them.

"Hi, guys. Hope you're hungry," she said cheerfully. "Did everybody have a good week?"

"It was okay," Justin replied.

Amber started to tell about her engagement, but she was too worried about her father. She tuned out the rock music her father was playing. Her father usually listened to an oldies station. He usually wore baggy pants and soft shirts.

Amber didn't like the way her father looked now. This whirlwind courtship was definitely not good for him.

Jennifer had picked a noisy place where the waiters served the food on roller skates. Loud rock music blared from the overhead speakers.

"All right!" Justin gave the restaurant a thumb's-up as they were shown to a table surrounded by a jungle of plants.

Amber and Justin each took a chair. Mr. Cantrell

and Jennifer squeezed side by side into the bench seat. An overhanging fern brushed the top of Mr. Cantrell's new hairstyle. He looked like he was wearing the plant as a hat.

Their waiter skated over to hand them menus.

"They have the best potato skins here," Jennifer said. "And onion rings to die for!"

"I love onion rings," Justin said, smacking his lips.

"Okay, we'll have onion rings for four to start," Mr. Cantrell said.

"Oh, not for me!" Jennifer said. "All that fat will go straight to my thighs. I'll just have a small green salad with the dressing on the side."

"I don't know why we go to restaurants if all you order is a salad," Mr. Cantrell teased. "You could have that at home."

Jennifer laughed. "I like the atmosphere! You guys get whatever you want. Don't mind me."

A plan slowly grew in Amber's mind. Her father was probably eating in restaurants all the time now, just to please Jennifer. She would convince him that eating at home was better for him.

"I'll have a small green salad, too," she said, lowering her menu.

Her father stared at her over his menu. "Amber, don't you want a hamburger? Or chicken strips? You love chicken strips."

"All that stuff is bad for you," she said. "Isn't that right, Jennifer?"

Jennifer was touching up her lipstick. "Well, it's okay once in a while." She closed the lid of her compact with a snap. "But everybody should try to eat healthy."

"Not in a restaurant!" Mr. Cantrell said. "That's the whole point of going out. To live it up."

Jennifer poked him playfully in the tummy. "You don't want to live it up too much. But you kids order whatever you like. This is your night."

Justin ordered a hamburger with all the fixings and French fries, but Amber stuck to her small green salad. She would rather have had chicken strips, but she would make the sacrifice to save her father.

The music was so loud it was difficult to talk. Jennifer and Justin moved their heads in time to the beat. Mr. Cantrell kept brushing the fern away from his hair. His hair stood up in little spikes, making Amber want to giggle.

She spoke up so she would be heard. "You know, it's bad to eat out in restaurants."

"That's the dumbest thing you've said in the last five minutes," Justin said scornfully.

"No, honest! It's fun and all, but the food isn't good for you. It's much better to eat at home and cook it yourself." Unfolding her napkin, she placed it primly in her lap.

"What is it with everybody tonight? Amber, I thought you liked to eat out," her father said to her. "You're always bugging me to take you to the pizza place."

Jennifer nodded. "You have a very smart daughter, John. She's right. Home-cooked meals are always best. You never know what you're getting in a restaurant."

Mr. Cantrell was beginning to sound annoyed. "Well, I wish you all had told me this sooner."

"It's okay, Daddy," Amber said. "It's fun to go out. But you should eat healthy things at home. Like what Mom cooks." To Jennifer she added innocently, "My mom is a great cook."

"I bet she is. My mother is a great cook, too. I love her pot roast." Jennifer sighed. "I'd die right now for her strawberry shortcake!"

"Daddy likes Mom's lasagna, don't you, Daddy?" Crossing her fingers, Amber asked, "Why don't you come over for dinner and have some good old-fashioned home cooking?"

Amber imagined what would happen. If her father came to eat, he would see that going out with Jennifer was all wrong. Maybe he would realize he missed eating with them at the round wooden table in their cozy kitchen. He'd realize he didn't need loud music or ripped jeans.

Maybe—Amber allowed her hopes to soar—her father would even fall back in love with her mother.

Her father unbuttoned his top shirt button, as if it was too tight. "Well, pumpkin, I don't think your mother wants—"

"Oh, it sounds like fun," Jennifer piped. "I adore homemade lasagna. And garlic bread!"

"My mom doesn't make garlic bread," Amber said heavily. She didn't want Jennifer to come along, too! That would be awful!

Later that night, as she was getting ready for bed, Amber picked up a snow globe on her dresser.

She shook the glass globe. Sparkly snow fell around a tiny Eiffel Tower. The globe was a souvenir from Paris, France. Delight had given it to Amber for Christmas. Amber liked it a lot.

Now she glanced up at a picture stuck in the mirror above her dresser. It had been taken a few weeks ago, at the last after-school meeting of the gymnastics squad.

Mrs. Holland, the gym teacher, had started an after-school gymnastics group for third-graders who enjoyed the sport. Amber, Mindy, and Delight had joined. But now it was softball season and Mrs. Holland had to coach the softball team after school. So the gymnastics squad was disbanded.

At the last meeting, Mrs. Holland had snapped a picture of Amber, Mindy, and Delight doing goofy headstands. Their legs were locked around each other's. Even doing headstands, the three of them stuck together.

Was a boy—even a boy like David Jackson—worth losing a friend over?

Amber went to bed, but couldn't go to sleep. She kept thinking about Delight.

She remembered the time Delight gave her back R.C., because she knew the raccoon was Amber's most prized possession. Then she remembered Delight's quick thinking when a little boy fell and hurt himself at Amber's house.

Delight was her friend. How could she forget all the fun times they'd had together?

Monday morning, Amber jumped on the bus. Mindy puffed behind her, trying to catch up.

"What is it?" she said to Amber. "Are you going to do something to Delight?"

"Yes," Amber said. "I'm going to make up with her."

Delight's stop was next. When Delight climbed on the bus, Amber eagerly pointed to the seat beside hers and Mindy's.

"I'm going to give David his ring back," Delight announced before Amber could say anything. "I don't want this to break up our friendship."

"Neither do I," Amber said emphatically. "We girls should stick together."

"You ought to teach that David a lesson," said Mindy.

"Yeah," Amber agreed. "I'm mad at him for what he did. Giving both of us engagement rings."

"David is a two-timer," said Delight. "That's somebody who goes steady with two people at the same time."

Amber felt a rush of anger. "Nobody two-times us! Mindy's right. We have to teach David Jackson a lesson."

"What can we do?" Delight asked.

Amber thought for a second. "We'll make him marry us. Then he'll be sorry."

Delight laughed. "Yes! He'll marry you first, then me. He'll have two wives! Won't that be awful?"

"No, wait!" Mindy cried. "Make him marry you both on the same *day*. At the same *time*!"

Delight bounced excitedly. "That way he'll have to admit he's been two-timing us."

"He'll be sorry he asked two girls to marry him," Mindy giggled.

"He'll be sorry he was ever *born*," Amber said firmly.

She couldn't wait until they got to school. David Jackson's days were numbered.

NINE

At lunch that day, the girls plotted the double wedding.

"How about making it tomorrow?" Mindy suggested. "I can't wait to see David's face when he figures out he has to marry two girls at the same time."

Amber shook her head. "Tomorrow's too soon. I want him to squirm a few days."

Delight passed around the cookies she had brought. "How about Friday?"

"Good," Amber said. "That way, David will have all week to be miserable."

As if on signal, all three girls turned to glare at him.

David was sitting at the table behind them. Uncomfortable under the intense gaze of three girls, he reached for his milk carton and missed.

"Hey, David," said Henry. "Your fan club wants you."

David spilled milk all over his tray. Henry choked with laughter.

Amber was pleased to see that David was flustered. Their plan was working already.

A few minutes before the bell, Amber noticed David taking his trash up to the garbage cans.

"Okay, Delight," she ordered. "Go."

Delight followed David to the front with her own lunch trash. As Amber and Mindy watched, she asked him a question. He shook his head, then slowly nodded in agreement. Delight skipped back to the table, her face flushed with excitement.

"It's all set," she said. "He said he'd marry me Friday, right after lunch. He didn't want to at first, but then he changed his mind."

The bell rang. Amber and Mindy hurried to the front with their trash as the rest of their class lined up to return to Room Six.

"Now it's my turn," Amber said. "Wish me luck."

She ran out of the cafeteria to catch up with David, who was walking with Henry.

"Go away, Henry," she said rudely. "I have to ask David something in private."

"You want to be alone with your *girlfriend*," Henry jeered at David.

David shoved him. "She's not my girlfriend."

"Oh, really?" Amber said. "Then who is?"

"Nobody," David answered hastily.

Henry still wasn't convinced. "You hang around girls too much, David. I think you like them all!" Then he ran off to bother Jonathan.

Amber and David were left to walk back to class alone.

"I'm really glad you told me I'm not your girlfriend anymore," Amber said sarcastically.

"I didn't mean it," David whispered. "I just said that because Henry was there. You know how he is."

Amber knew how Henry was. She also knew that she was being two-timed and she didn't like it one bit.

"So, I'm still your girlfriend?" she asked.

"Yeah."

"Your *only* girlfriend?"

"Yeah." But he hesitated before answering.

"We've been engaged long enough," Amber stated. "Let's get married."

David stopped, causing the kid behind him to bump into him. "Married?" he said with a gulp.

"Yes. I want to get married this Friday. Right after lunch." She looked quickly at David to see his reaction.

"Friday? After lunch?" he echoed weakly. "I . . . I don't think that's such a good day."

"What's wrong with Friday?" She peered at him. "Don't tell me you have something *else* to do that day."

"No . . . no," he stammered. "Uh . . . Friday's fine. You're sure you want to do it after lunch? Not in the morning?"

"After lunch," Amber said firmly. "Wear a tie." With that, she skipped ahead to walk with Mindy and Delight.

Her friends drew her eagerly into line.

"How'd it go?" Mindy asked.

"It's on!" she cried. "He's marrying me Friday after lunch, too!"

Delight glanced back. "Poor David. He has to marry two girls at the same time."

"Poor David!" Amber said scornfully. "He should have thought of that before he gave both of us engagement rings!" She didn't feel sorry for him in the least.

She wondered if David would show up in school on Friday. It would be just like a boy to chicken out and stay home, so he wouldn't have to marry two girls after lunch.

Thursday evening, Amber asked her mother to iron her white dress.

"I have to wear it to school tomorrow," she said.

Her mother unfolded the ironing board from the cabinet. "I didn't know you were in a special program. You didn't tell me."

"It's not a special program," Amber said. "But it *is* a special day."

She and Delight had arranged to wear white dresses and carry flowers. Amber decided that her white party dress would be her wedding dress. She couldn't very well go off to school with her mother's good lace bedspread wrapped around her.

There were no flowers growing in her mother's garden yet. The purple and yellow crocuses peeping through the dead grass along the front walk were too small to pick. Instead Amber found a bunch of silk flowers. They were just as pretty as real ones.

The phone rang while Amber and Justin were watching TV.

"If it's a girl for me, I'm not here," Justin yelled.

Amber looked at him. "Are you still fighting with your girlfriend?"

"It's over," Justin said. "I'm never getting mixed up with girls again."

Amber decided she wouldn't get mixed up with boys either. As soon as she taught David Jackson a lesson he'd never forget, she'd never have anything to do with boys ever again.

Their mother came into the living room. "That was your father. He was still at the office, so he couldn't talk long."

Amber's heart jumped into her throat. Did her father call to ask about coming to dinner? Was he bringing Jennifer?

"He invited you kids over to his place Saturday

night for a home-cooked dinner," Mrs. Cantrell continued. "Jennifer is doing the cooking."

"Jennifer?" Amber repeated. "I didn't know she could cook."

Her mother smiled. "Well, you'll find out Saturday night."

Amber put the dinner out of her mind. She had more important things to worry about. After all, she was getting married the next day.

On the morning of the big day, Amber put on her white party dress and her shiny white shoes. She asked her mother to fix her hair with a white ribbon.

"I want to look extra-pretty today," she said.

"Why? What's so special about today?"

Amber thought. She couldn't tell her mother the truth. What if she laughed like Justin did?

"We're having fish sticks for lunch," she said finally.

"You want to look extra-pretty for fish sticks?" Her mother pulled Amber's long hair back and tied it with the white ribbon.

"Yes. Make the bow big and fluffy."

Mrs. Cantrell brushed the ends of Amber's hair. "There. You look pretty enough to get married."

Amber grinned. That's just what she was going to do!

On the bus, Delight opened her coat to show Amber her white cotton dress.

"You both look great," Mindy remarked. "Wait till David sees you two. He's going to flip!"

At school, Amber and Delight strolled into Room Six together, carrying their coats. They were a vision in white.

The groom was sitting on top of Henry Hoffstedder's desk, talking to Henry about his pet snake. His face turned pale when he saw his two brides walk in the door.

"Hel-lo, David," Delight sang as she walked to her desk.

"Hi, David," Amber said meaningfully. "Guess what today is?"

"I don't remember," he mumbled.

"Maybe this will help you." She pulled the bunch of silk flowers from her knapsack and hummed a few bars of "Here Comes the Bride."

Henry looked puzzled. "What's the matter with those crazy girls today? Amber acts like she's getting married!"

David leaped off Henry's desk and hurried to his own seat, muttering something about finishing his math homework.

Amber put the bouquet on top of her desk, where David could look over and see it.

Mrs. Sharp called the class to order. After taking attendance, she told the students to open their cursive workbooks and copy a practice paragraph.

Amber licked her pencil and creased her workbook so it would lie flat. She glanced across the room and noted that David was hunched over his desk, writing with great concentration. He looked as if he never wanted the assignment to end.

After cursive practice, they did geography.

Mrs. Sharp pulled down the map of the United States. "Who knows where the mid-Atlantic region is?"

A few hands were raised. Mrs. Sharp looked around for students who didn't have a hand up.

"Henry," she said. "Do you know the answer?"

"Yeah. It's where we are."

"Could you be more specific?" she asked. "David, how about you? Do you know where the mid-Atlantic region is?"

Startled, David dropped his pencil. He bent to pick it up.

"David," Mrs. Sharp said. "Do you know the answer to the question?"

"The Congo," he replied.

Mrs. Sharp frowned. "Did you hear the question?"

"Didn't you ask something about Africa?" he said.

The class broke up laughing.

Mrs. Sharp rapped her desk with the map pointer. "Well, at least you're aware we're doing geography, David. For a moment there, I was worried."

Amber caught Delight's eye and grinned. David

was really getting rattled. The closer it got to lunchtime, the more nervous he became.

Next they had gym.

The weather was nice enough to play outside. Mrs. Holland organized a softball game. Amber and Delight were on one team. David was on the other.

When David came up to bat, Amber sang "Here Comes the Bride" from the outfield. David swung wildly and struck out.

Henry joined Amber in the outfield. "You're acting really weird today," he said suspiciously. "What's up with you and David?"

"None of your beeswax," Amber told him.

Later, she trapped David at the water fountain.

"How do you like my dress?" she asked.

He stared at the ground. "It's nice."

"Did you bring a tie?" Amber wanted to know.

"I forgot." His face brightened. "Let's get married on Monday instead. I'll bring my tie for sure. Okay?"

"No," she said. "I can marry you without a tie." As she walked away, she reminded him, "Twelve o'clock, on the dot."

When the bell rang, the third-graders lined up to go to lunch.

Delight stood behind David. She poked him in the ribs. "Remember. Twelve o'clock. By the garbage cans."

David stared straight ahead. He didn't answer.

Amber and Mindy got into the serving line ahead of David and Henry. Delight was next in line. David seemed nervous, having his two girlfriends so close to him.

As they took plastic trays, Mindy remarked loudly, "Oh, look, we have fancy cake today. It looks like wedding cake."

Behind them, they heard the clatter of utensils.

Amber pushed her tray along the rails, giggling. Her bridegroom kept dropping things today.

The cafeteria lady offered her a choice of fish sticks or macaroni and cheese. Amber and Mindy both took fish sticks.

Then it was David's turn.

"Fish sticks or macaroni and cheese?" the lady asked him.

David simply stared at her. His mouth was open, like a frog's. He looked terrible.

"Fish sticks or macaroni and cheese?" the cafeteria lady repeated impatiently.

Suddenly David flung his tray to the floor. He pushed his way back through the line and bolted out the door. Mrs. Sharp went after him.

"What's wrong with David?" Delight asked Henry with exaggerated concern.

He shrugged, taking a plate of macaroni and cheese. "Who knows? Probably this food made him sick."

Amber leaned forward so she could see Delight.

"Well," she crowed with satisfaction. "I guess we showed him."

Henry stared at Amber. "What did you do to David, Amber Cantrell? I smell a rat."

"That's just your upper lip," she said.

There would be no wedding. But Amber was happy. Her plan had worked.

Chapter

TEN

David Jackson did not come back to class after lunch. Mrs. Sharp said he had gone home sick.

Amber knew the truth. David wasn't sick at all. He was too chicken to face the girls he had promised to marry. So he had skipped out.

The class cut out shamrocks for their St. Patrick's Day bulletin board.

As her scissors edged around green construction paper, Amber felt content. She had done a good job of teaching David Jackson a lesson. He wouldn't mess with Amber Gillian Cantrell for a long, *long* time.

It was during Errand Time that she heard the first remark.

Amber was thirsty, so she used her Errand Time to get a drink of water.

Three fourth grade girls were gossiping around the water fountain in the hall outside Room Six.

"My sister told me about something that happened during lunch today," said one girl.

"What?" asked a second girl.

"Some kid in Mrs. Sharp's class was going to marry his girlfriend. At lunch! Can you believe it? This kid had two girlfriends. His other girlfriend found out and she decided he was going to marry her, too. The kid ran off. He didn't want to marry two girls at once!"

"Boy, those little kids are *wild*!" commented the third girl.

"I wonder who that kid's other girlfriend is? She sounds cool."

The first girl replied, "My sister said the girl had really long hair, but she didn't know her name."

The fourth-graders started to walk away.

Amber bent quickly to get a drink of water, feeling a glow of pride. *She* was that kid's other girlfriend, the one they said was cool. Those older girls were talking about *her*.

If fourth-graders knew about the wedding-that-never-happened, who else did?

She soon found out.

On the way to the library later that afternoon, their class passed a group of second-graders.

"Look!" said one of the little girls. "There she is!

That girl with the long hair."

She pointed to Amber. The other little girls with her stared at Amber.

"She's the one who made that boy run away at lunch today," said the girl in a hushed tone. "I saw her."

Another girl looked admiringly at Amber. "She must have scared that boy awful bad. I want to be like her when I'm in third grade."

Mindy was wide-eyed. "Everybody in the whole school is talking about you, Amber! You're famous."

"I guess I am," Amber said proudly. She liked the way the little girls had looked up to her, as if she was a hero!

In the library, Henry Hoffstedder marched up to the table where Amber was reading.

"You tried to get David to marry you and Delight," he said accusingly. "You made David run away. You ought to be ashamed."

"He had it coming," Amber said coolly.

"He may never come back!"

Amber was unconcerned. "He shouldn't have two-timed me."

"Just like a girl!" Henry yelled. "Girls are weird!"

"Not as weird as boys!" Amber retorted.

Miss Maddox swooped down on the table. "Henry, this is a library, not the playground. Amber, keep your voice down."

Henry went sullenly back to his seat. Amber walked over to the shelves near the librarian's office to choose another book.

Miss Maddox was talking to Amber's teacher. " . . . heard about that ruckus in the lunchroom," the librarian was saying.

"Yes," said Mrs. Sharp. "Apparently there was almost a wedding."

"*Two* weddings, from what Henry tells me. What a way to get back at a boy!" Miss Maddox chuckled. "The girl who thought of that plan is a real doozy!"

Amber didn't know what a doozy was, but she was glad everyone in the school was talking about her. For once, Henry's legendary mouth had done Amber a favor. She was famous!

Back in Room Six, Mrs. Sharp paused by the blackboard, studying her class. Amber wondered who her teacher was looking for. Then Mrs. Sharp's eyes settled first on Delight, then Amber.

"Delight Wakefield, Amber Cantrell," she said. "Please come see me. The rest of you work on your math assignment."

Amber slowly left her seat and walked up to Mrs. Sharp's desk. Delight looked just as nervous. Were they in trouble?

Speaking in a low tone, Mrs. Sharp said, "Henry told me about the little scene in the cafeteria. I don't know exactly what is going on between you two and

David Jackson, but David went home very upset. He was crying when he left."

Amber felt a twinge in her stomach. She had just wanted to teach David a lesson.

Mrs. Sharp spoke to Amber. "I believe you are the one responsible for this. Am I correct?"

"It was his own fault!" Amber exclaimed. "David was two-timing me and Delight. We just taught him a lesson."

Mrs. Sharp's voice was stern. "Friends should be loyal, but do you think what you did was fair? You humiliated David. And now everyone knows what happened. How do you think David feels?"

Amber looked down at her shiny white shoes. "Not very good, I guess. But he shouldn't have given us engagement rings."

Mrs. Sharp nodded. "I agree David used poor judgment. But this was a private matter between the three of you. You should have settled it quietly, like ladies and gentlemen, not turned it into a show for everyone to see."

Delight finally spoke up. "I'm sorry, Mrs. Sharp. What can we do?"

"Apologize to David," Mrs. Sharp said. "He's the one who was hurt. You may go back to your seats now."

Amber went back to her desk.

Mindy glanced up from her math paper. "What happened? Are you in trouble?"

"Sort of. We have to apologize to David Jackson. He's upset because of what happened today."

It was Friday. She wouldn't have to face David until Monday, three days away. If he came back.

She took out her math book and stared at the page of fractions. Her mind was too jumbled to concentrate.

Mrs. Sharp had said Amber had to apologize to David, but Mrs. Sharp should make David apologize to *her*. After all, she was the one he had two-timed.

But somewhere deep down, she really *was* sorry for what she had done. She had never meant to make David cry.

Amber sat on the sofa in her living room, holding a vase of carnations. She was waiting for her father to come pick up her and Justin. Tonight Jennifer Donovan was cooking dinner at her father's apartment.

The carnations were for Jennifer. Mrs. Cantrell had bought them on her lunch break.

"I still don't see why we have to give Jennifer flowers," Amber said to her mother. "She never gave us anything."

"I told you, it's a courtesy," Mrs. Cantrell said. "If you are invited to dinner, you bring something to the hostess."

"Mindy comes over for dinner all the time," Amber said. "She doesn't bring anything."

"That's different. Mindy's practically family." Her mother pushed back the drapes. "Here comes your father now. Remember, Amber, no matter what Jennifer serves, try to eat a little of everything."

"Even if I don't like it?"

"Even if you don't like it." Mrs. Cantrell walked them to the door.

Jennifer was not in the car this time. Justin got into the front seat next to Mr. Cantrell, because it was his turn to ride up front. Amber climbed into the back seat.

"Where's Jennifer?" she asked.

"Back at my apartment, cooking up a storm," her father replied. "I have no idea what we're having. Jennifer wouldn't let me in the kitchen all afternoon."

On the drive to Maryland, Amber looked out the window and chewed her thumbnail.

The other week in the restaurant, she had tried to show her father how unhealthy it was to eat out all the time. She wanted her father to come over and eat a home-cooked meal her mother had fixed. Then maybe her father would come over more, and forget about going out with Jennifer Donovan.

Well, they weren't going to eat in a restaurant. But now Jennifer was fixing the home-cooked meal instead of Amber's mother. Jennifer was probably a great cook. She seemed to do everything well.

Amber didn't know how to save her father. Lately, all her plans had backfired.

Up front, Justin was punching radio buttons. "Where's that tape Jennifer gave you?"

Mr. Cantrell groaned. "No rock music, please. Jennifer and I went out dancing last night. I'm still deaf from the band."

Amber glanced at her father in the rearview mirror. He looked tired. This whirlwind courtship really was bad for him. She would have to do something!

She pretended she was Amber Gillian Cantrell, Third Grade Legend. What would a folk hero do to solve this problem? Folk heroes were very strong, but they were also very smart. Sometimes folk heroes could make things happen just by thinking clever thoughts.

Maybe, Amber figured, she could think bad thoughts and make Jennifer ruin the dinner. It was worth a try.

At her father's apartment, soft music played on the stereo. The dining room table was set with a white cloth and elegant, long-stemmed glasses Amber had never seen before.

Mr. Cantrell hung up their jackets. "Jennifer brought over her own china and glasses. She really wants this to be a special dinner." He smiled proudly.

Amber glanced around the apartment. It was neater than usual. Jennifer must have cleaned, too. Then she noticed something on the bookcase. It was just what she needed! She hoped her father would let her borrow it.

Jennifer emerged from the kitchen, wiping her hands on an apron. "Hi, guys! Dinner will be ready in a few minutes."

Amber held out the vase of carnations. "These are for you."

"Oh, aren't they pretty! They'll look perfect on the table." She set the vase in the center of the dining room table, then scurried back into the kitchen.

It was time to get to work. Amber sat down and started thinking bad thoughts. She squeezed her eyes shut and thought, *Dinner, be awful. Dinner, be terrible.*

Jennifer came out again with a silver tray. "Appetizers!"

Amber opened her eyes and stared at the brown lumps on the tray. Her thoughts had worked! Jennifer's appetizers looked terrible.

"What are these?" she asked doubtfully.

"Mushroom caps stuffed with spinach and feta cheese." At Amber's blank expression, Jennifer laughed. "Feta cheese is made from goat's milk."

"Goat's milk! Yuck!"

Her brother kicked her on the shin. Amber realized she had been impolite.

"I mean, goat's milk. Yummy!"

Mr. Cantrell took one of the appetizers. Gobs of

cheese fell off the mushroom before he could pop it into his mouth.

"I guess I used a little too much feta," Jennifer said. "How do they taste?"

Mr. Cantrell made hand signals because he could not speak.

Justin boldly popped a mushroom cap in his mouth. Then he made a horrible face that Amber could see but Jennifer could not.

It was Amber's turn. She had promised her mother she would sample everything. Taking the tiniest bite possible, she managed to swallow only mushroom, avoiding the spinach and goat cheese filling. Her bad thoughts were definitely working. The appetizer tasted awful.

Dinner was ready. They all sat down at the table. Jennifer made several trips to the kitchen, bringing out platters.

"Something sure smells good!" Mr. Cantrell remarked.

Amber sniffed. Nothing smelled good. But just to make sure, she kept up her bad thoughts.

Dinner, be terrible. Dinner, be awful.

"I hope everyone likes stuffed eggplant," Jennifer said cheerfully.

Amber had never had stuffed eggplant so she didn't know if she liked it or not. But she had a feeling she wasn't going to be asking for seconds.

Jennifer began passing dishes. "To go with the main course, I made artichoke hearts in black bean sauce, rice with mangoes and chili peppers, and homemade potato bread." She beamed as she handed Justin a basket. "I used my roommate's bread machine."

Amber didn't like anything on her plate. The eggplant was slimy, the artichoke too spiny, and the smell of the rice made her sick. When the breadbasket came to her, she pounced on it desperately. At least she could eat bread!

But when she tore open the loaf, the inside was hard and gummy. She couldn't eat the bread either. Her bad thoughts were *really* working.

Mr. Cantrell ate a few bites of rice, then put his fork down quickly. He gulped water like he was lost in a desert.

"Not used to chili peppers, I guess," he said, wiping his streaming eyes with his napkin.

"You haven't touched your eggplant," Jennifer accused.

Mr. Cantrell picked up his fork reluctantly. "I'm not a big eggplant fan. But it's good," he added hastily.

"Where's the meat?" Justin asked, sorting through the mess on his plate.

"It's in the eggplant," Jennifer said. "I used ground turkey instead of ground beef. Red meat is bad for you."

"Ground turkey?" Justin repeated. "Turkey all ground up?" His voice sounded funny. Then he started coughing. He excused himself from the table.

"You're not eating," Mr. Cantrell told Amber. He tried to put more black bean sauce on her plate. But the spoon was stuck in the bowl. The bean sauce was like glue.

No one was eating except Jennifer. To cover up this fact, Mr. Cantrell began talking about the movie he and Jennifer had seen the other night.

"The preview of that new movie looked great," he said to her. "Want to catch it this weekend?"

"I can't," Jennifer said. "My college roommate is coming. We're going on a twenty-mile bike ride. Want to come along?"

"No, thanks," Mr. Cantrell said. "My bike . . . uh . . . has a flat."

When Jennifer went to get dessert, he pushed his plate away gratefully.

"It's not like Mom's cooking," Amber said.

Her father nodded. "I miss your mother's cooking."

"Then why don't you come to dinner next Saturday?" Amber said boldly. "She's having something you like. Lasagna!"

"I don't know, Amber . . . your mother might have plans."

"No, she doesn't! I know she wouldn't mind if

you came over." She didn't know, but she would worry about that later.

Just then Jennifer returned, carrying a large soggy pie covered with icky green things.

"Kiwi tart!" she said, cutting a huge slab for Mr. Cantrell.

When Jennifer called Justin in for dessert, Mr. Cantrell leaned toward Amber. "Tell your mother I'll be there," he promised.

Under the table, Amber crossed her fingers. *This* plan had to work!

On Monday morning, Amber walked into Room Six. She glanced nervously toward David Jackson's desk. Would he be back? Or would he stay home because he still felt terrible?

He was back. He sat at his desk, quietly looking at a book on snakes. Even Henry Hoffstedder wasn't talking to him. Amber thought David looked embarrassed, as if he wanted to be anywhere but school.

Amber paused. Mindy and Delight were right behind her and they stopped, too.

"We have to apologize to him," Delight said to Amber. "Mrs. Sharp said so. I want to anyway. He looks so sad."

"You go first," Amber said, nudging Delight. "You sit in front of him."

Delight went over to her seat and put down her knapsack. Then she turned to David. Amber was too far away to hear her speak, but she appeared to be apologizing. David nodded, clearly accepting her apology. He looked even more embarrassed though.

Amber went to her own seat. She should go right over and apologize, too. But something held her back. She *was* sorry for making David upset. But he had hurt her, too. She had thought he was her boyfriend.

Mrs. Sharp called the roll.

"Your folk legends are due one week from today," she announced. "That's next Monday. I'll give you time to work on them this week. We'll begin this morning, instead of having Monday morning Press Conference."

Mindy took out her notebook and pulled out several sheets covered with her smeary handwriting. "So far I've got six pages," she said. "How long is yours?"

"I haven't even started yet," Amber replied.

Mindy gawked at her. "We've been working on our stories for weeks! Why haven't you started?"

"I can't think of an idea."

Something always bothered her whenever she tried to write. First she was worried about her father's whirlwind courtship. Then she was excited about being engaged. Now she was wondering how she could apologize to David.

"I can't believe you don't have an idea," Mindy said to her. "You're always loaded with ideas."

"Yeah," Amber said glumly. "And lately all my ideas have gotten me in trouble."

Then she thought of an idea that wouldn't get her in trouble. She would write her apology to David. That way, she wouldn't have to face him.

While the rest of the class worked on their folktales, Amber scribbled a letter to David:

Dear David, it said. *I'm sorry for what I did. I'm sorry I made you cry. But I'm still mad. And when I get mad I stay mad. Yours truly, Amber Gillian Cantrell.*

During Errand Time, Amber dropped the note on David's desk on her way to the water fountain. When she came back to the room, she saw that David was reading her letter. He folded it quickly and stuffed it in his math book. He didn't look up at her, even though he knew she was standing there.

Amber trudged back to her desk. He wasn't going to accept her apology. Now what would she do?

Next the class had library period. Amber walked down the hall in line with Delight and Mindy. David was in front of her. He did not turn to joke with her the way he usually did.

They passed a bunch of fourth-graders going to the gym.

"There's that girl," one of the fourth-graders said,

pointing at Amber. "The one who tried to make that boy marry her during lunch."

"Stay out of *her* way," another kid remarked, laughing.

Amber could see David's back stiffen. He had heard, too. Now he would never forgive her.

Feeling miserable, Amber sat down alone in a corner of the library and tried to read a book about Mike Fink.

Someone tapped her shoulder.

She looked up, surprised. It was David.

"I got your note," he said.

Amber stared at the book in her lap. "I guess you didn't like it."

"No, I liked it." He hesitated. "I just . . . I'm sorry, too, for . . . you know."

Amber understood what he was trying to say. "I thought you liked me."

"I do."

"Then why did you give Delight a ring, too?" she asked.

"Because . . . I like her, too," he replied, flushing.

"You can't like two girls at once," Amber told him.

"Yes, you can." Then he added, "But I liked you first."

Amber remembered the way David had sneaked around her house to spy on her Valentine's party. He liked snakes, but he liked girls, too. He wasn't mean and loud like Henry Hoffstedder.

"You know what?" she declared. "I think you're a romantic."

"A what?"

"A romantic," she repeated. "It means you love love. My brother's a romantic, though you'd never know it most of the time. My father's a romantic, too. Lots of guys are. There's nothing wrong with it."

David flushed again. "If you say so."

Amber thought he looked cute, going all red like that. "I'm not mad anymore," she told him.

"I'm not mad anymore either," he said. "Can we forget about this girlfriend-boyfriend stuff?" He held out his hand. "Friends like always?"

Amber took his hand and shook it. "Friends like always."

But as David walked away, she got that warm, vegetable-soup feeling in her stomach. He really *was* the cutest boy in class. Maybe she would let him be her boyfriend again sometime.

When the librarian came over to check on her, Amber had a question.

"What's a doozy?" she asked. "Like, if you called somebody that."

"Oh, a doozy is a real character," Miss Maddox replied. "One-of-a-kind, in a crazy, wild sort of way."

Amber chewed her thumbnail thoughtfully. She was beginning to get an idea.

"What time is he coming?" Amber asked her mother.

"I've told you a hundred times, he'll be here at six." Her mother opened the oven to check on her cake.

Amber looked at the clock. It was now four-fifteen. Her father was often late.

Going into the living room, she dialed her father's apartment in Maryland.

He answered on the second ring.

"Daddy?" Amber said. "This is Amber. I just wanted to make sure you're coming."

"Dinner is at six, right? I'll be there."

"Daddy, you're supposed to bring the hostess a little present. It's a courtesy."

Her father laughed. "I know, pumpkin. I have something for your mother. Is there anything else? I have to get ready."

"Yes, would you bring me something, too?" Then she told him what she needed. Her new idea depended on it.

Amber could hardly keep still waiting for the evening to begin.

The aroma of lasagna filled the house. Mrs. Cantrell had baked a chocolate cake for dessert and was tossing a fresh green salad when the doorbell rang.

Amber hurried to open it. She crossed her fingers.

Her father stood on the doorstep. He was not wearing those awful torn jeans or the stiff new jean jacket. Instead, he was wearing tan pants and a soft blue shirt. His hair was combed sideways again. He looked like his old self.

"Daddy!" Amber cried, hugging him.

"You'll soon be stronger than me." He handed her a plastic bag. "I can't imagine why you need this, but here it is."

Amber ran to her room and stuffed the plastic bag behind R.C., who was sitting on her pillow. Then she ran back to the living room.

Her mother was opening a fancy-wrapped box. "Chocolates! My favorite kind!"

"I didn't forget," Mr. Cantrell said to her. "I haven't forgotten what a great cook you are either."

"And I didn't forget that lasagna was *your* favorite," Mrs. Cantrell said, laughing.

Amber was thrilled with the way her parents were getting along.

"Did you see the way they looked at each other?" she whispered excitedly to Justin.

"It doesn't mean anything," he said. "Don't get your hopes up."

It was strange having her father over for dinner. He sat in his usual place at the head of the table. But he didn't act the way he used to when he lived at home.

Amber expected her parents to talk about report cards or plumbing problems. Instead, they talked about movies and books and laughed a lot. It was like they were on a date.

"This dinner is delicious," Mr. Cantrell praised. "The salad is wonderful and the lasagna is, too! I can't believe I've had three helpings."

"Have more," Mrs. Cantrell urged. "Simple food is always best, I think."

"Not an eggplant in sight," Justin said.

This time Amber kicked him under the table. But she giggled, too.

"So Jennifer isn't the best cook in the world," said Mr. Cantrell. "But she tried."

"Well, she's very young," said Mrs. Cantrell.

Mr. Cantrell looked at her. "Okay, point taken. Jennifer is sweet, but I doubt we'll be seeing much of each other anymore. She has other interests."

Amber's heart lifted at this news. "It's not good for you anyway," she said.

"What's not good for me?" her father asked.

"That whirlwind courtship. It was bad for your health."

Her father stared at her for a second, then

laughed. "I think you're going to be as wise as your mother."

When dinner was over, Amber and Justin offered to wash the dishes so their parents could talk.

The next day, a basket of white carnations arrived for Mrs. Cantrell.

Amber sniffed the flowers. "Are they from Daddy?"

"Yes," her mother answered, setting the flowers on the table. "They're pretty, aren't they?"

"Does this mean that you and Daddy are going to go out again?"

Her mother put her hands on Amber's shoulders. "Amber, this is just a thank-you for a nice evening. That's all."

"Aren't you and Daddy going to be boyfriend and girlfriend?" Amber asked hopefully.

"The flowers don't mean anything," her mother said gently. "Except that we are friends."

"Just friends?"

"Just friends."

But Amber didn't believe it. She still felt in her heart that her parents cared for each other.

That night Amber finally began her folktale assignment. She wrote about the Doozy. The Doozy was a giant third-grader who could make boys tremble when she walked by and make her father's young dates cook terrible meals.

The Doozy was one-of-a-kind, an original, a real character.

A lot like Amber Gillian Cantrell.

She finished her paper, then copied it over. It was almost time for bed.

Amber took the plastic bag from behind her stuffed raccoon. Her father had put directions in the bag. It didn't take her long to figure out how to use the device.

The next day, Amber turned in her folktale paper. Mrs. Sharp promised to read and grade everyone's papers that very day.

Amber received her paper back after lunch.

Mrs. Sharp placed it on her desk so Amber would see the big red A. "How does it feel to be a legend in your own time?" she asked Amber with a smile.

"It feels great!" Amber replied.

She *was* a legend. Everyone in Virginia Run Elementary knew about Amber Gillian Cantrell. She was as famous as Paul Bunyan and Johnny Appleseed. No one would ever forget that Amber Gillian Cantrell, that doozy girl, had set up the wedding-that-never-happened.

But just to make sure, Amber took out a strip of pink plastic from her knapsack. Her father's label maker had come in handy.

The plastic strip had raised letters that read *AGC—Doozy.*

She placed the strip on the underside of her desk and pressed it firmly until it stuck fast.

Years from now, some other third grade girl would sit at this desk and feel the strip underneath. The girl would get all excited when she read the initials on the strip and realized someone famous had once sat there.

And that person was none other than Amber Gillian Cantrell.

Tales From Third Grade

Don't miss a single minute of third grade!
Join 8-year-old Amber Cantrell as she copes with changing friendships and family situations — and discovers how much fun third grade can be!

#1 Who Needs Third Grade?	0-8167-2989-1	$2.95
#2 Third Grade Stars	0-8167-2995-6	$2.95
#3 Why Are Boys So Weird?	0-8167-2991-3	$2.95
#4 Third Grade Detectives	0-8167-2993-X	$2.95

Troll Associates, 100 Corporate Drive, Mahwah, NJ 07430

Please send me the books I have checked above. I am enclosing $_____ (please include $2.50 for shipping and handling). Send check or money order—no cash or C.O.D.s. Allow 4-6 weeks for delivery.

Name_____

Address _____

City _____ State _____ Zip _____